CONTRACT FOR LOVE

MARGAUX FOX

1

I feel the heat pulse through my skin. The slow uncomfortable drip of sweat runs down between my shoulder blades.

There is a moment when it comes to running, I call it the point of clarity. Where my body adjusts to the push and finds this almost serene equilibrium of present and not present.

The point of clarity is the feeling that got me hooked on running; the first time it happened it felt like an out-of-body experience. Where all of my being was throbbing with life but my mind was almost detached, my thoughts not confined to the actions, just a complete separation.

My coach told me that not all athletes feel that

way; for many, they have to endure that pain, that physical exhaustion with no relief, and it instantly made me appreciate my mind more. It was a few years later that I realized that running had become more than just a passion and an outlet, it had become my addiction.

I focused and built my entire life around athletics. Rising through the ranks from Juniors into the adult women's teams, living for the meets, a dedicated focus on training for the next event, qualification, medals. What they don't tell you though is that talent, ability, dedication…it doesn't mean so much if you don't have a team, sponsors, money. Everything costs so much, and the moment you leave college you get an abrupt awakening that you have to do it all yourself.

Track and Field is just not where the money is at. Unless of course you are a superstar. Or unless of course, you are the 'right' kind of athlete to attract the big sponsors.

I'm neither. I'm the nearly athlete. Good, but not the best; I don't have the bundle of Olympic Gold Medals. I'm attractive and clean living, I know I look good on the track and in the gym, but I'm not the girl the sponsors want on their ad campaigns- I don't have the instagram presence and the ability to self promote that they want from me.

This is why at 28 years old I share a downtown apartment with three others, work at a hotel bar six nights a week, and do everything I can to secure more money to fund more events and continue following my dream.

I feel my calves really burn as I power up the steps to the fourth floor, that final push to make it through the front door is always a killer, but one that really makes me feel that ache in my legs. As my key turns in the door, I can hear the shower running and I try my best to hide my disdain as I make my way down the hallway, tapping slightly too loud on the locked door.

"Milly, it is 2.05 pm. This is my scheduled bathroom time!" I shout through the door.

"Whattt!?" she shouts back even though I know she heard every goddamn word and I KNOW she knows this is my time.

"I said ...IT IS NOT YOUR FUCKING SHOWER TIME. YOU HAVE TWO MINUTES BEFORE I CUT THE WATER."

I know it sounds harsh. But we had carefully mapped out four, thirty-minute slots when it came to the shower times that worked around everyone's schedules, especially when it came to work times, and the thing was, I had to adjust my run time to the middle of the day, which generally meant facing the most people in the park and the blazing hot sun in the summer. So, when Milly—who had demanded her slot with zero amount of compromise then proceeded to take everyone else's when she felt like it—it well and truly pissed me off.

A good five minutes later she pads out of the bathroom, still dripping, with steam covering the walls and windows. "Jeez, Alexa. You weren't here so I figured I had time to nip in. No need to get all salty." I bite back a comment and instead dive into the newly freed bathroom so I can feel the pound of cold water against my aching limbs.

I have forty-five minutes until my shift starts at the Luxe Hotel. Luckily, I live about three minutes away, which makes up for the time it takes for me to adhere to their stringent appearance code. Front-facing staff are hired as "career models" and I use air quotes with the title very sarcastically. They include the name *model* in the job title for the simple fact that it gives them some scope to fire us based on appearance. For all other intents and purposes, I was just a barmaid in a posh hotel.

Due to my focus on nutrition and training for

my track career, the weight and size rules are never an issue. I weigh the same, right down to the pound, as I did when I started there six years ago. My uniform is perfectly cared for by my Grandmama. I drop my shirts, a-line skirt, and stockings off Monday morning and collect them Tuesday afternoon when I have my weekly lunch with her. The biggest issue for me is hair and makeup; I'm sporty-femme as opposed to girly-femme. Luckily, my immediate boss is not a complete asshat. After six years, and watching the rest of the staff come and go with a myriad of issues, he accepts that my eyeliner may not be on fleek but I'm never late, never sick and I always do a great job.

We have a few approved hairstyles to choose from, though I generally opt for the sleek-up pony, and makeup rules have been filed away in my head as something I will never learn. I simply do the same thing every single day and hope it passes the appearance test.

My long, thick, dark hair is wrapped up high on my head, drying in my towel as I survey myself in the mirror. I know physically my body is at its optimal peak. My chin gets its sharpness and my cheekbones get their angles from my mother. My dark hair really contrasts with my big blue eyes, making them pop against the paleness of my skin tone. That is the feature people most notice and take a second glance at. That is why I have a front facing job in one of the top London hotels that usually only employs models.

I sponge foundation onto my face, it's so light against my skin I may as well not be wearing any, but I know I will be thankful for it when 2am comes and the dark circles really shine through under the mood lighting. A smear of pearly eyeshadow and a flick of mascara is the most adventurous I get. I have seen a hundred YouTubes and endless TicToks on how to apply false lashes, how to blend four shades across your eyelid for a dark, mysterious smokey look ... but whenever I try, I just look like a clown.

So, I stick with what I know, the only real flash of sexy is the smudge of red across my top and bottom lip. It isn't exactly in keeping with the code, but with my dark curls and alabaster skin, it changes my whole face, giving me an edge and making me look a lot more sophisticated than I perhaps feel. In reality, as soon as I see myself in the mirror with that signature smear of red lipstick, it feels like a mask, an identity I can hide behind so I don't have to admit that this temp summer job I had laughed about years ago is now my actual career.

I slip my feet through the sheeny fabric of my stockings and then slide into demurely sexy black kitten heels. The good thing about working in a fancy hotel bar is that the uniform is all provided. I only have to take care of it, which I do, but the quality is high which makes it easier. Wearing heels is not a favorite of mine, but luckily these are just as comfy as some of my trainers.

I grab my bag and purse as I whirl out the door, annoyed at myself that I didn't make anything to eat. I would have to go beg Jorge in the kitchen for something when my stomach started to rumble.

I take the back streets so I can enter the hotel through the staff entrance. It is frowned upon for staff to take the front door anyway and it's always hit and miss as to who might show up at a hotel of this stature. The last thing I want ten minutes before my shift is to get tangled in a paparazzi storm because someone famous has showed up. And those guys are absolutely ruthless. Not famous? Then you're totally disposable and be prepared to take an elbow in the ribs so they can get past you.

The Luxe Hotel is the epitome of indulgence. I

don't even take cash at the bar, it is card or room only—we don't handle something as dirty as money. I usually work alone except on the weekends or if there is an event. There are some regulars, mainly businessmen, and when I say regulars there isn't a pattern to when they prop up the counter, it's more just returning faces. The décor is expensive. Cream leathers, polished glass, and mirrored surfaces. My bar is kept perfectly stocked with exclusive expensive spirits that would cost my paycheck for a bottle of.

My job takes no thought these days. I can whip up a Sidecar cocktail without skipping a beat. I have perfected a Mojito to the point that I could make it in my sleep. If the bottles are half an inch out of place, my fingers know when I reach for them. The part that requires thought is the people side of things. Tips make this job pay way better than terrible. Some nights I've earned more in tips than from a whole months paycheck, but it requires effort to get tips like this. It often requires giving more of myself than I might wish to give. Perhaps some people have a natural ability to read others. To know who wants to flirt, who wants to chat, who needs silence, who looks like they needed silence but are actually craving attention...

It isn't a talent I possess. (or perhaps want to go to the effort of developing.) My default is nonchalance. I do my job with impeccable calm precision. I don't raise an eyebrow or stumble at the most ridiculous requests I receive, I soothe the egos, flutter my eyelashes, and offer the softest of smiles.

A few hotel guests have tried to seduce me. In the beginning, I was flattered. Everyone who stays here has a bank balance that would make my eyes water; they are used to being the center of attention, when they speak people listen, so for people like this to notice little old me... I found it surprising. But as time went on, some of the people that flirted with me one month wouldn't notice me the next, and that's when I realized I wasn't anything special to them. I wasn't memorable or remarkable, just there, present, and an option.

I've slept with two guests over the years, which, compared to other staff that work here, is barely worth acknowledging. Both times it was a one-night-only thing and I had zero regrets. There had been a moment where a charming smile and the promise of more had worked on me. Where I had felt the flutter between my thighs and I had acted upon it.

It was a risk in terms of it being against hotel

policy, however, there is also a very unofficial look-the-other-way policy if it kept guests happy and returning and no possible whiff of scandal or litigation. Both times there had been no risk of either, the first guest was some Danish or Dutch banker who I have never seen again and doubt I ever would. But for one night those piercing blue eyes and blonde curls kept me captivated in her silky, fresh-pressed sheets.

The second had been slightly more of a risk as she was, at the time, a musician who was on the cusp of making it. That wasn't the appeal, I didn't care about that, but what had caught my attention was her sad eyes and lost smile that seemed to tell far more about her than her half-assed lyrics ever did. However, she only rode the cusp and never actually did make it, and it wouldn't surprise me if she were now somewhere in the world in a similar position to myself, thinking about the days when she was almost someone no one would forget so quickly.

Both times the sex was pretty good, there had been a spark, a chemistry, and a feeling of satisfaction but nothing that had rocked my world. If anything, I had taken more of a kick with the hotel toiletries I had rehomed the next morning before I had ducked out of the staff exit and made my way back to my humble abode.

I slip into the staff area and push my few bits into my locker before giving myself a final look over in the mirror. Same as always, perfectly pressed but a little imperfect around the edges.

The first few hours of my shift are always generally quiet. I'm supposed to use this time doing a list of menial tasks like polishing the glasses or chopping fruit but I rarely do. I keep everything neat, clean, organized and stocked so I usually eyeball the TV that plays in the corner minus the sound. I've become a pro at lip-reading over the years.

The bar in the hotel is clever, it's not like the dining area or lobby, which brings the outside inside. In the bar, there are no windows, it is constantly evening, made with the illusion that no matter what the actual time is, it is perfectly acceptable to be drinking. It makes time distorted. Some days I can glance at my watch with incredulity that only an hour had passed and other days be pleasantly surprised that I'm nearing the end.

Today is to be one of the better days. It seems like I haven't been here long at all before Robbie comes through to give me thirty minutes to take my break. I sneak through to the kitchen and bat my eyelashes at Jorge who pretends to shoo me out before piling my plate high with pasta Bolognese and hot melted cheese.

"Oh, Jorge, this is the best thing I have ever tasted."

He looks over the shiny steel countertop with a raised eyebrow as though that was ever in doubt. It is one of the things that I love about living in London. It is a cultural clash of ethnicities. Jorge is Sicilian and even though he has lived here most of his adult life, he still curses in Italian and rolls his Rs in a way that makes my heart flutter.

A lot of the hotel staff are from other countries. There is no main place. Eastern Europe, the Med, the hospitality manager is German, and I like that; I like living and working in a place where cultural differences are not only accepted but encouraged too.

I amble back to the bar with thirty seconds to spare on my break, but Robbie is already waiting to dash off, and I know why the moment I enter because I can hear the bustle of the room filling and the sighs of impatience as people have to wait for their order. He isn't as efficient on the bar as me and we both know it.

"What can I get you, Sir?" I greet the first person who catches my eye and begin to prepare his order within about seventeen seconds flat, but that elicits a soft tut from a woman perched at the end of the bar. After I serve him his drinks and charge them to his room, I make my way over to her.

"What can I get you, Ma'am?" I ask her softly waiting for her to turn and make eye contact with me.

I am definitely fluid in my sexuality, tending towards women. I can appreciate a beautiful woman as much as I can an attractive guy. I've been with women and men over the years, never anything serious, never anyone who sparked anything more than a passing desire in me.

As the woman at the bar turns to face me, I have to hold my gasp. Not because I recognize her, because of course I do, but because I have never seen a woman so beautiful in the flesh.

Her thick, dark red hair is piled up high on her head and tumbled in an effortless grace that frames her face. I know she is over forty, but her skin has a beautiful translucence to it. The light kiss of a tan seems to emit a radiating glow from her high cheekbones, and her eyes are so green they look like an instagram post with a filter. But, this is no filter, this is real life. Her makeup looks minimal, but I can tell it has taken time to perfect the look of nearly nude, and she wears it beautifully. It makes her look younger, fresh faced and carefree, which if her recent exploits in the newspapers are anything to go by, she most certainly is not.

"I'll take a cosmopolitan. Virgin. But make it look like it is loaded with the good stuff." She grins at me, a beautiful smile with neat white teeth and glossy pink lips, as she swivels in her stool to face me and greets me with a long rolling southern drawl.

I embellish, making a show as I shake the cranberry juice and soda, pouring it into a frozen glass so the condensation runs in a smooth line down the stem. Next is a twist of orange juice and a squeeze of fresh lime. I pour it to perfection. I serve around the same amount of mocktails as I do cocktails as a lot of extremely wealthy people seem to avoid touching alcohol. I imagine it has something to do with no limits. If you could afford to drink yourself into oblivion with no consequences, what was to stop you from doing it once, twice, three times a week until it developed into a problem.

However, sober people are also more likely to notice if it tastes like shit, which is why I usually put a little more effort into the non-alcoholic versions. But that is not the reason I'm giving *the* Dahlia Dante my best show here.

I slide a black coaster embedded with gold flakes across to her and place the glass dead center so the glistening golden flecks will shimmer in the prism of the glass bottom. It looks fancy, it costs about a buck to make. In fact, the coaster probably costs more than the drink, but that isn't the point. The point is the show.

I watch as Ms. Dante reaches with elegant fingers and red manicured fingernails. Her soft palm curls around the stem and she looks up at me under long thick lashes as she takes the lightest of sips. Barely a drop passes her lips but it is enough for a taste.

"Perfection. Almost worth the wait." Her voice is gravelly. She winks before standing. "Charge it to my room—850."

Her heels sink into the carpet, but she doesn't need them for height anyway. She is tall and I find my eyes running hungrily over her body. The exquisite curves of her waist and hips are just as good as they look on screen, maybe better. Her breasts are barely held in by a deep emerald halter-neck dress that bunched at her hips as she sat but now falls to her ankles, covering her diamond-encrusted stilettos. The dress is slit up to the upper thigh on one side. It flashes enough to show her thighs are perfectly toned, but as she turns to walk away there is no denying the sensational curve of her peachy ass. I am staring. I know it, but I can't help it.

"She is really something in the flesh," murmurs a guy at the other end of the bar, and I nearly agree with him until I realize he is actually talking to his companion and not, in fact, me.

The rest of my shift drags and I'd be lying if I said I didn't check the door to see if each new guest was, in fact, a returning Ms. Dahlia Dante. I was already googling her as I clocked out and left through the back entrance making the few blocks home.

Photos online just do not do her justice at all.

Her absolute radiance in real life outdoes any photograph I could find.

She's a household name, sure, but I realise I don't know much about her history.

She had been thrust into the limelight from a young age as part of the child star crew of some hit American teen trash show. After that, her personal life had become a public soap drama in itself. She had been emancipated from her parents at fifteen and since then her entire life had been run and managed by her manager.

In her mid-twenties, she had married some older country singer, who I personally had always thought was gay, but there had been no denying the chemistry between them when they arrived at events. He had shone and she had sparkled and could do no wrong... Until they had very privately separated a few years ago.

The problem when you have built your life and fortune around a very public life, the media doesn't love it if you decide to keep the juiciest gossip private. The power couple, the Southern Sweethearts, the ultimate American Dream, separated and no word on why.

Of course, the rumors started. Even now, years later, one of the top hits on Google is speculation that Jayden had left her because Dahlia cheated on him with his drummer. I could find zero substance to the article other than pure conjecture and speculation, but it was a clickbait title that earned the trash papers some more ad revenue.

Jayden Ellis had walked away from his divorce with not so much as a tarnished shoe. Wasn't that always the case though with famous, attractive men? It must be the woman's fault... And Dahlia's career had certainly paid a price for it. She went from A-list events to B-list movies to C-list, to straight to Netflix releases quicker than a has-been reality star, and she didn't really deserve that fate as she had always had a beauty and a talent on screen that made her characters raw and real.

As I tumble into bed and throw my work clothes in the wash bag ready for my Grandmama on Monday, I'm still flicking through images of Dahlia Dante on my phone, but the more I look, the more I feel like she is far more beautiful in reality. There's just something about her that I can't shake. As though those piercing green eyes have seen straight into my soul.

2

"Come on, Alexa. Push through, push through. That's it, get into your stride... focus." Andy, my coach, is getting frustrated. I can hear it in his voice. See it in my time. I'm off my game; my focus is distracted and I need to be in it. I need to go into the zone where nothing else matters except pushing my body to the limit.

"Okay. Let's call it for today," he adds with a sigh as I drop to the ground and try to catch my breath. My limbs are burning. My lungs are on fire. I couldn't get myself into that space where I could push past the pain and so every inch of my body seems to be screaming in protest.

Andy drops to a crouch next to me and grabs

my ankle, raising my calf in an unusual gesture of kindness as he squeezes hard on my calf. I feel the sting of pain then instant relief in my muscle as his thumb works out the spasm. "You only have a few weeks, Alexa, until the 10k meet. And you know, I don't want to say this is it. It is never *it* if you are still focused, improving, dedicated. But you are not going to get many more chances like this." I watch as his beautiful dark brown skin glides over my tan shin so his fingers can work their magic.

He is attractive and reminds me of the actor Jamie Foxx a little bit. He's been my coach for nearly ten years and even though he was in his late thirties when I met him, he still could pass for late twenties; he seems to have not aged a day in all that time. Not like me; I've gone from the awkward teen, rebellious college kid, straight through to the person I am now. Which is probably a chaotic mix of all those things.

I manage to find my voice and gasp out an, "I know." Which I do. It isn't last chance saloon, but I need to make the big leagues now or I'll need to accept the fact that I'm too old and this is now my hobby, just a pastime, and I'll need to always have an alternative career. A proper job.

"Are you okay? You seem distracted?" he asks softly, glancing up at me with deep dark eyes.

I nod. "I am. I just, need to focus. You know."

He nods and switches legs. "You should hit the pool; you need to give your muscles a little break from pounding the pavement. Are you still doing the strength and conditioning programme in the gym religiously?"

"Conditioning and weights every other day," I confirm, and he smiles as he gives my calf a final squeeze before standing. He holds out his palm to give me a hand up, which I happily take.

"Good. You have it all there, Alexa. The talent, the drive, the speed, the fitness. I know you can hit the times you need to to make it big, you just need to pull it all together. I know that it has been a hard road for you and I tell my other clients about you, your determination- you are someone who has what it takes. It isn't about winning all the time; it is about perseverance and fucking hard work. That is what makes athletes, not the medals, the commitment. Don't forget that."

"Thanks, Andy," I say sincerely and he nods.

"I'll see you next week. Meanwhile, do your strength and conditioning programme, get some swimming in, and focus on what is ahead."

My weekend passed uneventfully and other than work, gym, swimming, and running I had nothing worthy to talk about. I took the bus out of the city and dropped my washing off at my Grandmamas and spent my one day off out running errands and chores before meeting up with some friends for a few drinks.

My job was always a source of interest to them. Especially as most had them had sold their soul to the devil and took on regular office jobs, which made each day as gray as the next but gave that all-important regular paycheck so they could afford their very own and private tiny loft space in the city.

I was seen as the wild one. The one who had never really grown up, and I got where the idea came from but it wasn't exactly true.

Mostly, I couldn't be less wild.

I could have gone into the world of insurance, taken an admin job, worked as a receptionist until I got a promotion to PA. But those kinds of jobs just didn't give me much flexibility when it came to my training. Whereas at the hotel, I could double up shifts, switch around, and take my time when I needed it to make it to track and field meets. Not that I made it to that many anymore, but that had always been the intention.

Plus, my hotel job was motivational too. I knew that by staying at the hotel job, it felt like it was just a side job. It felt like I hadn't given up on my dream of being an athlete, whereas the moment I took on the nine- to-five, mentally I would be admitting that I hadn't made it. That I wasn't good enough, and whilst that day was coming nearer and nearer at an alarming pace... I wasn't quite there yet.

So back to my friends. They lived for the details, wanted to know who was in staying at Luxe, who was hooking up with who, who was secretly gay, who was now T Total. I usually had no issues with telling them because I owed these people nothing and let's be honest, who were my friends going to tell. But I found myself biting my tongue when it came to Dahlia Dante. I didn't want to spill her secrets. I didn't want to talk about her. So, I passed it off as a quiet week and got back to hitting the tequilas.

I felt like shit the next day and the bus didn't help, but I knew my Grandmama's cooking would be just the thing I needed to make me feel alive again.

I know what you're thinking. At my age, I should be able to clean my own clothes and cook my own meals, and the truth is I could. But this was our thing, you know. Our routine. She wasn't so good on her feet and found it hard to come and see me race anymore, but this was her way of being present in my life, and I looked forward to it every single week. It was never a chore. Never an "Oh, now I have to go out of the city." It was my escape and my precious time with the person who loved me the most in the world.

"Hey, Grandmama," I sigh as I fall through the back door and collapse at the kitchen table.

"Hey, pumpkin. Your clothes are all done. I folded them and put them in the holdall in the room over there. How are you doing? Dinner will be done in a few minutes. Would you like a drink? Some tea? Water? Soda? I got the zero zero stuff you like."

I smile up at her. She is my father's mom. My parents had both died in tragic circumstances when I was young, before I could even remember them, and Grandmama and Grandpapa had brought me up. A lot of people gave me the pity eyes when I was growing up, but the truth is I didn't know anything different. And I was super lucky to have grandparents who loved me like that.

Money was an issue; both were on the cusp of retirement and in no way prepared to raise a child, and they kept the life insurance money to pay for my college, so we had all learned how to live with less. What I lacked in material things, though, was more than made up with love, attention, and affection. Most people I knew had issues growing up, parents that fucked them up or situations that changed them, became defining moments in their lives that shaped them into different people.

It would be easy to think I was the fucked up one, poor little orphan, Alexa, but that couldn't be further from the case.

My childhood was perfectly vanilla. There was no drama; I went to a nice school, had a couple of good friends, a loving home, and faux parents that adored me and did all they could for me. I never thought of the what if. What if there had been no accident. What if I had been raised by my own parents, because honestly, I grew up really happy so what would be the point in changing any of that.

My grandpapa passed away just after I graduated. I feel like he held on to see that, but in reality, old age was waiting in the wings, and whilst we all fought against it, it was just his time. My grandmama took comfort in the fact he would be with my dad. She saw it as almost a happy thing, finally back with his son who had been taken too soon.

I don't know if I believed in things like that really, but I was pleased the thought gave her some comfort and didn't break her. That the good positive thoughts meant she had a way of finding peace and an ability to carry on.

We chat and eat. I tell her about my track event next month and about drinks last night. She tells me the street gossip and about her plans for the week. It's normal and I leave with my holdall, a full stomach, and a smile on my face as I head back into the city for my shift.

Arriving at Luxe, I follow the same routine as I always do. I slide in behind the bar and eyeball the TV and I look pretty and smile nicely when required, but don't get much done. Guests come and go but overall it's quiet. Tuesdays are often a slow shift. I take my break, but still being full from lunch, I just sit out back and scroll on my phone as

I watch the thirty minutes tick by before ambling back in to make my way through the rest of my shift.

As Robbie runs off, I notice that the previously empty end of my bar is now occupied by the very person I had hoped I would see again.

"Well, here she is," says the red-haired movie star with a grin as I make my way over. "I was hoping to get another of your delicious cocktails."

She sits delicately perched with her elbow on the polished bar counter and her chin perfectly rested against the palm of her hand. She isn't dressed up tonight, instead, she's in more comfortable clothes—a tee and some slacks—but even from over the bar I can see they cling to her figure in a way that makes them seem like a polished outfit in themselves.

"Yes, ma'am. The same? Or would you like to try something different?" I ask with a professional edge to my voice trying to cover any hint of unprofessionalism I may feel.

"Surprise me." She smiles and her voice rings with a light tinkle that makes my skin tingle. I take my time preparing her a piña colada. It is the best virgin cocktail, in my opinion, because it still has those bursts of flavors that you can enjoy without the burn of alcohol.

I place it lightly on the black and gold coaster and move away to give her space. I find her difficult to read as to whether she wants to interact with me or not. Everything about her invites me in, but her quick exit last week makes me cautious that she's probably only waiting for someone else or has other plans.

"This is absolutely delicious. Makes me glad I gave up the booze for the first time in forever." She doesn't raise her voice to combat the distance between us, which means I have to move back, closer to her to reply.

"It is my favorite too when I'm on a no-alcohol regime- which is often."

She raises her eyebrows questioningly. "You have no alcohol regimes but you work behind a bar?"

I laugh. "Yes. I actually rarely drink anyway; it messes with my fitness plans, but there are months when I have to go zero."

She nods. "You are a PT?"

"God no." I laugh then remember where I am. "I mean, it's not my thing. I just like to run, that's all. It's all for me, I don't try and motivate others...

far too much pressure." I laugh again. She smiles softly, her peachy lips curling a little at the sides, but her eyes are like chasms, endless pools that give nothing away.

"Aren't you going to ask what I do?" she says, leaning back in her chair whilst her fingers toy with her straw. Slowly stirring her drink. I stumble a little bit. I mean, I know exactly what she does, who she is. Everyone does. Should I pretend...

"I'm just fucking with you. Everyone knows who I am. I used to think that was a blessing. Now I am not so sure if it isn't some kind of curse ..." her voice trails off and I don't say anything. "Anyway." She smiles, it is dazzling, and gives me a light but fake laugh. "I am here for a few weeks. I have some promos. Some evenings I have to go out and play nice, but others... I am at a loose end, so I'm sure I will be propping up your bar. In a totally respectful, southern kinda way."

It is my turn to smile at her. I fix her gaze with my own. "I would be honored to have you here propping."

The next night, I look for her again and feel the tingle straight between my thighs as I catch sight of her perched on her usual seat.

She looks beautiful in a simple black dress that would do nothing for most people, but on her... it looks a million dollars. It fits her to perfection and makes me instantly want to buy one even though I know for a fact it isn't the dress that makes her look so good; it was the other way around. Her body seems made to make clothes look good, every smooth curve of her seems perfectly drawn, and I bet designers adore her. Her proportions seem perfect to me. She is delicate and graceful, my eyes scan every part of her, wishing I could undress her. The way her breasts and ass are curved and full oozes femininity. Her wrists and hands are elegant and her fingers long, and I imagine them playing a piano. Or playing a woman's body; the thought of it assaults me suddenly, and of course, I'll volunteer mine. Her fingernails are neatly manicured and painted red. I can't take my eyes off her.

Of all those things, it isn't her body or her hands that catch my attention the most, it's her eyes. I have never seen eyes so clear and green, and the soft red sheen of her hair only brings out their sparkle more, lighting up her whole face. I can see why she is such a famous sex symbol, why men are so drawn to her, but the softness, the kindness in her smile, is what makes me like her too. She is the kind of woman that men want to fuck and women want to be friends with.

Unless you are me and you and want both.

I can tell by the slight smudges of her makeup and the stray curls that fall casually and sensually from her updo that she is not on her way out but rather returned from wherever she had been and as if she can read my thoughts ...

"I just got back from a full afternoon of promos. You know, I don't think they care about the movie at all. They just keep me there to see if I will make a mistake and say something that will look good splashed across a front page," she says with a soft sigh as I approach and I feel bad for her.

"Drink?" I ask gently, and she snaps out of her thoughts.

"Oh hon, I am sorry. I hate to be one of those people ... like, *oh my life is so bad because I am famous*. I'm lucky, I know I am lucky. Just some days, I feel the vultures circling. You know?"

I nod as I start to fix her a drink. I don't know,

of course, but I can take a guess at how it would feel.

"I mean, I don't know anything different. This has been my life for as long as I can remember. But I do wonder what it would be like to just go to a grocery store without being recognized, or re-wear the same clothes without being photographed, maybe eat a burger in public ... take a drink ... go on a date..."

I finish her drink and place it in front of her, and she meets my eye as she continues, "... sleep with a stranger ..." Her eyes sparkle with mischief, and I feel myself take a deep inhale.

I imagine the impure thoughts I'm having about her this second are written all over my face. How I would love to make her forget all that bullshit and just lose herself in me. In a moment of pleasure. She is clearly so used to being in control of all her actions... I wonder if she would enjoy being directed, guided, told what to do. If she would obey.

I watch her skin flush across her chest, her pupils dilate a fraction as she leans in closer and I smell the sweetness of her perfume mixed with the scent of her, knowing she can smell me too. I feel her breathing me in too. My head spins faster and I feel intoxicated.

"Bourbon on the rocks. Room 586," a man calls. His voice is close but the words sounded distant. I want to ignore him, to focus on Dahlia, but I can't. The moment is broken, but it happened and we both felt it.

Over the next few nights, Dahlia did prop up my bar. Each night when I returned from my break, she was there on the end waiting for me in her slacks and tee with her red hair swept up into a messy bun. She never gave anything away though she was there for hours. Sometimes she was content in the silence. I felt her eyes on me, watching me work. I saw her watching other guests and making polite small talk with the men who tried to approach her. But, she didn't look at them the way she looks at me.

Other times, she talked and talked. It was hard to get anything done around her. Her soft southern drawl kept me enraptured. I am not someone who says that much anyway but that didn't faze Dahlia in the slightest; she was happy to be the one to keep the conversation going.

But I noticed how guarded she was. She told me things but they were never personal, never about her or her life. Always her opinions on things, a view from afar, but nothing that felt real. I couldn't put my finger on it but for how open Dahlia was… all I could feel was an impenetrable wall.

She isn't gay—but then again I'm not totally sure that is how I'd define myself—but there is a spark between us. I feel it whenever I see her. At first, I assumed it was one sided. Coming from only my desires and my want to touch her, feel her, taste her. Of course I do. Probably everyone does. Because of how she looks. Because of who she is. Because of the sensuality she exudes.

But I caught the way she looked at me once when I was working, I felt her gaze skim over my body, her eyes were glazed with lust, and I was sure then that she felt an attraction to me too.

The intensity for me has only built. My total intrigue into her grew with each passing moment and I now find myself obsessed with the details of our conversations. I can't stop thinking about all the things she said and more so all the things she didn't say.

With men, they are rarely shy in an invitation to their rooms. In fact, they seem to think that this is my first rodeo and I have never had a guy casually offer me a key card as he leans over and whispers the room number. (It happens all the time.) I smile and do my best to act surprised. I sometimes wonder if they wait for me in their room or if they know by my eyes when I take the card that I never had any intention at all of actually meeting them.

With women, the dance is different, and for all of her confidence and show, I felt like Dahlia was secretly hiding her low self-esteem, and I wondered if that would stop her from ever asking me to spend time with her privately. I wasn't shy; I was confident in my body and who I was, but I didn't want to cross a line with a hotel guest. Especially when she was so high profile. However, as the week sped by and I knew time was ticking for her leaving, I decided to bite the bullet.

"You know I can't make you a cocktail tomorrow night," I say the following Sunday as I serve her up a mojito.

She looks at me in mock shock. "You mean you are leaving? Running away? Gone and never to be seen again? Ooooh, this is good," she adds with a satisfied moan as she takes a deep sip of her drink.

I appreciate the satisfied moan and it makes me imagine other things.

I laugh. "No, it's my day off," I reply as I feel the slightest of flush to my cheeks at her gasp of pleasure. She leans in a little closer with a playful grin.

"Yeah, I figured they might let you take, you know, one night off a week."

I nod and then lean in a little closer. "I do get the night off, and I don't have plans. So, if you want a cocktail, I can still make you one. If you wanted."

Dahlia is an actress; if she has any surprise at my offer, she doesn't let a flicker of it show. She acts as though my proposition is exactly as she expected and responds in the same way as if I had asked her about the weather.

"I have a nice bar in my room I am sure we could make use of. Why don't you come up tonight and see if we need to get it stocked with anything special in preparation?"

I nod with a smile and continue with what I was doing, but my mind is in overdrive. I haven't shaved, I certainly am not wearing my best underwear, and I really would have preferred to have taken a shower before... Oh, what am I thinking?

Making drinks, flirting, and perhaps making out doesn't mean we have to do anything more. Just because I want that to happen doesn't mean it has to be tonight. There is time.

The good thing about us both being women is that whilst platonic friendships with guests are not encouraged it is definitely less frowned upon than fucking the guests. It is much easier to sell a 'friendship' between two females as purely platonic. That means when I take the elevator up after my shift to Dahlia's penthouse suite, I am much bolder and obvious with what I am doing, because I feel like if I am more brazen with our friendship it would seem less suspicious.

Dahlia left the bar a couple of hours earlier so it is just me. I'm still in my work skirt, but I pull on a sweater over my blouse so I look a little less like staff and a little more casual. I only tap twice on the door before it swings open and Dahlia greets me with a coy smile. Her eyes meet mine and the look we share is loaded.

"Come in, quick. I don't want to get my favorite cocktail connoisseur sacked."

"Oh, it's okay, we are allowed to be friends with the guests as long as we respect the boundaries."

She's wearing the same clothes as earlier, but

she has touched up her makeup and let her hair down. It is so long, it cascades in thick red curls over her shoulders and down her back. I almost reach to touch it, wanting to feel the softness in my palm as I wrap her locks around my hand.

"Is that what you want to do, Alexa? Respect the boundaries?"

She asks me casually as she perches at her private bar. She is staying in the largest suite I have seen in the hotel. It's like an apartment, the social area being nearly the size of my entire apartment. Everything is expensive, the finishing oozing in class and elegance.

"I don't particularly care for hotel boundaries. I am much more interested in what yours are."

Her eyebrow raises an inch but she doesn't comment, instead, she moves, making her way around the bar.

"How about a little roleplay? You can sit pretty on the stool and I will make you a drink. Alcohol or virgin?"

I sit on the stool and watch her as she slides behind, her fingers already reaching for a glass as her eyes scan the bottles weighing up her options.

"Either. It's my day off tomorrow, I can have one. Or, I can stick with no alcohol if you prefer."

I'm surprised to see the spirits lined up. For many alcoholics, it would be a trigger but she seems unfazed. She must have read the confusion as I take in the bottles.

"Oh, I'm not an alcoholic. It's just something my manager tells people in case he ever needs to explain away a situation. God forbid I break the rules sober. Much better if I did it while intoxicated. Then he can whisk me away to some spa under the ruse of rehab until the whole thing blows over. I haven't had an alcoholic beverage in public in six years, but I keep my own bar well stocked for occasions such as these."

She begins to make us a cocktail and I watch her with interest. She has a flair, a casualness to knowing exactly how she likes it and has no need to deviate from that method. Her nails are short but perfectly painted, which I like. Many women opt for long nails these days, and whilst they look chic, they are hazardous. Particularly for fucking women, which is where I want this to go. I want her fingers inside me, and short neat nails are reassuring that she might know what she's doing with her elegant fingers.

I don't follow what she is adding to the drinks. I just watch her move, seeing how her wrists turn inwards as she twists the shaker. Her fingers point on the metal tongs as she takes ice from the bucket and adds it to the glasses. She is mesmerizing and I am enthralled. I can smell her, dusky roses and sweet cinnamon tones that would taste like Christmas on my tongue. I want her.

"Here." She smiles as she hands me the glass, and I'm oh so careful to make sure we don't touch, keeping my fingers steady as I accept the drink and take a deep sip. It's nice, too sweet for me really, but drinkable, and I would have put a good bet on the fact that if you had more than three you wouldn't be walking home in a straight line.

I settle it back on the bar, glancing up to watch Dahlia drain her glass and place the empty one beside mine. She seems nervous, there is an edge to her usual confidence. I guess she is taking a huge risk having me here. I could be anyone. I could sell her out to the press and even though I know myself and know I wouldn't, she doesn't know that. It's as if she read my thoughts.

"I want to let my guard down with you, Alexa, but I have learned that trust should not be given easily and even though you may say right now the things I want to hear... inevitably those feelings can change like a turn of the tides and I leave myself open to being vulnerable. A place I can't afford to be. I think that we both know I desire you. As you desire me, but before I can act on those feelings, I need to protect myself and my reputation. Do you understand?"

I am receiving a speech. I can tell by her tone, the words do not flow naturally but instead are thought out, rehearsed, and recited from memory. I wonder how many have heard them. How many have done what I am about to do? I suppose that this is the risk when you want to experiment as a famous person, and it is the draw for someone like me, to fall into a secretive high profile luxury world with a celebrity.

I look up and meet Dahlia's deep green eyes. I hold her gaze, reading the messages I choose to see rather than the ones she's actually giving me.

The truth is, I want her and I am willing to play by her rules to have her.

"Yes. I understand."

3

My worries about shaving and clean underwear turned out to be very premature. I finish my drink and whilst we flirt a little longer, it is clear that we aren't going to move any further forward tonight. Instead, she asks me to come by her room tomorrow at eleven to discuss our situation further.

On one hand, I am pleased to leave; it makes me look better on the hotel CCTV, and I definitely want to take my time in preparing for alone time with Dahlia. But on the other hand, discussing details of the possibility of our fucking seems cold to me.

I don't know if it was the adrenaline crash or what, but the moment I got home and laid down I passed out waking groggily at six the next morning feeling completely out of it. I decide to get up and head straight over to grandmamas to drop off my washing. She won't be concerned about the early time; she is used to me leaving them on the doorstep with a note if an early morning run fits my schedule.

It is my turn to fuck up the shower routine, but I try to time it the best I can and work in super-fast time, meaning my rushed work with the razor leaves me with a cut on my ankle that won't stop bleeding.

I'm not a really girly girl. I've always spent all of my non-working time in sweats, joggers, running gear, and Lycra. I own a few nice outfits for the times when I need to make an effort, but I'm not exactly sure what someone should wear to an eleven o'clock meeting with a celebrity who they want to hook up with.

I opt for branded, tight-fitting black joggers that make my ass look good with sneakers and a tight-fitting black tee; I want to feel comfortable and like myself. I run the brush through my hair and let it down, dark and shiny waves around my shoulders. I consider makeup but it just isn't me, and if Dahlia wants a woman like that, she could find a million of them, so I'm happy to push indecision to one side and just be confident in myself and who I am.

I debate between the front and back exits of the hotel and opt for the front. I am, after all, a friend of a guest, and not an employee today. I don't know if it is the shades, the confidence, or my hair being down, but no one even notices me. They let me straight through as though I belong, and as I ride the lift up to the 85th floor I realize that it's because I feel like I could belong.

I don't even need to knock; the moment I approach, Dahlia is already there opening the door and welcoming me inside.

I'm thankful I opted for casual, as she has done the same. In black yoga pants and a loose shirt, she looks warm, feminine, and soft. Her hair is still down but a little messy, slept in. She looks less perfected, which in my eyes makes her infinitely sexier, and I wonder how often she ever gets the chance to let her hair down and just enjoy life without worrying how she looks.

My bet is not so often.

I enter and am surprised to find us not alone.

On the sofa area sits an older, balding man; his shirt looks expensive but ironed poorly and he has an air about him that I find off-putting. A detached coldness. I feel his gaze and know he is trying to fit me into a box. Judging me based on only my appearance and choice of clothing.

"Take a seat, Alexa. Would you like some tea?" Dahlia asks.

I begin to answer, but Mr. Suit cuts straight through me.

"Let us get this out of the way first, shall we, Dahlia?" It's posed as a question but it is anything but, and Dahlia nods, sitting down in the armchair between us as though she is now the mediator.

Mr. Suit pulls out a leather document holder and opens it slowly before letting his thumbs work through the paperwork.

I eye him suspiciously.

"As you know, Ms. Sharpe, my client is a very famous and very successful celebrity who has a high level of public scrutiny. I am aware that neither of you has had any physical interaction but that you may intend to, and it is for this reason we have scheduled this meeting today. In order to protect my client's reputation, you will need to sign these documents." He slides a wad of paper over to me that has my name, number, address, and tax information plastered all over the front, which instantly makes me feel uncomfortable.

"How do you know—?" I start, but he cuts me off again.

"I make it my business to know. I understand that this is not a normal occurrence for people outside of the world of celebrity, but I can assure you it is how things are done in the world that Ms. Dante lives in. She cannot afford to take any chances. If you can read through the paperwork and sign where indicated, you and my client are then free to engage in any sexual activities you choose. As you can see on page five, we outline and list some of my client's preferences and what we mean by certain terms. By signing this agreement, you acknowledge that you will not discuss my client with anyone. No one is to know any details of your liaisons, that includes specifically any members of the press—during or after the fact. For recompense for agreeing to the terms of this agreement, you will receive a financial incentive of one hundred thousand pounds that will not only serve as a thank you for your discretion but a binding term of the agreement that you will not disclose any information now or in the future in regards to time spent with my client or her sexual orientation or preferences."

I take a moment to let all that sink in. It doesn't seem real. I have to sign a contract? I'm going to be paid to keep my mouth shut? A hundred thousand pounds? What on earth are these sexual preferences of Dahlia's? What world am I even living in?

"I know it is a lot, Alexa," Dahlia says softly and breaks my current trance of incredulity. I nod to her, words failing me because I know that Mr. Suit is completely right; these things might be very common practice in their world but they most certainly aren't in mine.

"You are going to give me money? Doesn't that make me some kind of...?" I let my words trail off as the statement is left unsaid. Dahlia starts to shake her head, and I watch Mr. Suit keep his lips firmly closed for the first time.

Dahlia is the one who speaks. She looks up at me. "No. The payment makes it part of the contract; it is what binds it, if you like. Right now, it seems like an insult and you may want to argue that you don't want it. But think about the future, think about the things it can give you and then if you don't want it, you can give it away, a charity or something. Do something good with it. Help someone you care about. I don't know. Put it to good use. I have plenty of money; it might seem like a lot to you, but it is nothing to me."

I stop and try to take a deep breath. The thing is that even now I am totally attracted to Dahlia. I can feel her energy in the room like a magnet. When she moves, I sense it. I have never seen a person that oozes so much raw sexual energy, and I feel like I see it in waves through the air. Calling to me.

Sex is just sex. I don't do relationships but I do enjoy sex. I know that she will be electric sexually and I will enjoy every single inch of her. But we have never even kissed. I don't know anything about her sexually and maybe I am signing myself up for a fall.

Then I think to myself... So why does it matter? I can sign the papers, if nothing happens, I won't lose anything, and it's not like I would tell someone anyway; I am such a private person. I pick the papers up and begin to thumb through the pages once more. I pretend to know what I am looking at, but if I am being really honest my only reference for this is totally fictional from a Mr. Grey and his 50 shades. I never rated those books, and I have an idea his story was entirely unrealistic.

Not like this. This is my real life and a very wealthy famous woman is offering me money and a contract for sexual services.

My eyes catch page five and my fingers hover ... *Marks left on Ms. Dante's body must be able to be covered ... no breath play but gags may be used ... dominance permitted with the guidelines of sexual pleasure only ... no photographs when tied ... shared only if agreed previously ...?*

The words swirl in my head.

"Dahlia, I don't know ..."

"We are unable to discuss the contents of page five further, Ms. Sharpe, unless you first sign the documentation." Mr. Suit cuts through me like a knife and I find my curiosity explode. I have experimented a little in my time, and I'm certainly not a prude, but the things listed... I have only seen them in porn or read about them in erotica. I have never tried them myself. I know I am naturally dominant when it comes to sex. I know what I like, what I want, and it makes me feel good when I claim that from the other person. I like to tease, to edge, and then take what I want. But I would never categorize myself as a Domme. I have never been anything further than assertive, but even now as I think about it... my thoughts jump through images of Dahlia naked and bound and entirely at my mercy, Dahlia naked and on her knees begging to please me, Dahlia bent over and opened up for me, and I find my body responding to them, feel the tingles between my thighs as I...

My gaze drifts upward to meet Dahlia's. I can see her thoughts are there too. Her skin is slightly flushed, her pupils dilated, and I wonder if I were to brush the tips of my fingers over her panties if I would feel a hint of her wetness as she thinks about me taking everything I want from her.

I reach for the pen as I fix my gaze on hers. I want her to watch me, to read my mind and my thoughts as I sign, to know I'm not doing this for money or a quick fuck. I'm doing this because I want to have her in every way I possibly can. And as if she can read my mind, I watch her cheeks flush deeper as her teeth run lightly over her lower lip in nervous, needy excitement.

As soon as my name is etched and my pen lifted from the paper, I see her visibly relax as though she can finally let down her guard with me.

"Okay, Ms. Sharpe, we can now go through—"

Mr. Suit begins to talk, but I'm kind of fed up with his presence.

"You know, I think Dahlia and I can talk through it together. I've signed the agreement so there isn't anything more for you to be concerned with right now."

It is a dismissal, and though I can see he wants to argue with me, he has lost my attention and Dahlia's too. With nothing more than a nod, he collects the signed papers from the table.

"Very well then," he adds stiffly. "This is your copy and I highly recommend you read through them. Ignorance won't get you very far in court if you were to break any of the agreement due to unknowingly not following one of the rules." He stands slowly, and as a professional person with a set of morals, I try my best to hide my disdain for him but it definitely is not easy to do. "The money will be in your account in a couple of hours." He nods to Dahlia and then leaves. I don't move until I hear the lock click on the door and then I settle back in my chair.

It is strange but I feel no nerves. It's almost like I hadn't realized what I wanted, what I craved until I read those words in the agreement and saw Dahlia visibly giving herself over to me. But now those images have passed through my mind and I can't switch them off. I can only see her, me, us in various tangles of sexual exploration, and I want it. I want it so fucking bad.

Dahlia eyes me; she is waiting, perched at the edge of her seat. Waiting hopefully.

I feel like I need to take this moment to be entirely honest with her.

"I need to be totally honest with you. I have never done most of this- the BDSM stuff. I don't know what I am doing. I can only follow my instincts and trust in you to guide me and communicate with me. To tell me if I am going in the wrong direction." I am open with her, earnest. I want us to have that trust. An open book and understanding of what we are stepping into.

She looks at me with a serious look on her face and her green eyes are clear and ever lovely.

"That is all you can do. I have books. There are websites where you can learn. I know some clubs. You will learn. Most of it will come naturally." Her voice is slow, her words are deliberate and her southern drawl is something I will never tire of. "I will show you what I like, but I can feel the dominance in you. I know you have what it takes to take me where I need to go. I can see exactly what you

4

As an athlete, I am very aware of myself and my body. I can usually tell you my own heart rate after a few seconds, and I can lower it quickly with specific breathing techniques. I understand the effects of hormones, especially adrenaline, and I can control and manipulate my endorphins to boost my performance as and when necessary.

The moment Dahlia rises from her chair I feel my heartbeat quicken, and I can see it in her longing eyes that she needs the reassurance that I want her. The public façade of Dahlia Dante is dropping faster than the rain in England, and I am reading her constantly to see what she needs from me.

I let her see my desire, I let her feel the heat of my body as she moves closer. Then I take control.

My heart rate lowers as I breathe efficiently and settle my mind, calming the surge of adrenaline that pounds in my veins so fast it is enough to make my head spin. I can feel my panties resting against my pussy but I don't give in to it, I don't move my hips or seek relief. Instead, I watch Dahlia with undivided attention.

Her fingers fall to her hips and she casually lifts the hem of her loose tee upwards. My first glimpse of her body is smooth, creamy skin and full, rounded breasts that spill over the cups of her black t-shirt bra. There is no padding; she doesn't need it.

Her yoga pants rest just below her belly button, which is pierced. The stud is simple and from it dangles a small sparkling butterfly that catches the light in any which way she turns, and I have no doubt it is a real diamond that sparkles on the butterfly.

Her thumbs run along her midriff as her hips begin to sway, but before she pulls down her pants, she spins on the ball of her right foot and turns away from me, so as the black fabric peels away it rides the curve of her ass giving me the perfect view of her soft, peachy skin.

Fuck. I want to take a bite.

But it isn't just her ass. Her panties rest just below the Venus dimples of her lower back, and my eyes roam upwards, hungry to take in every single inch of her. I watch how her bouncy red curls fall against her freshly bared skin. The way they swing when she moves her hips and how toned her legs are as she lowers to her ankles to take off her panties.

She turns back to face me and I let my gaze start at her perfectly painted toes, over her delicate ankles, and up her defined, graceful legs. She reminds me of a dancer in some ways. Her legs and feet definitely do. There is an elegance and femininity to Dahlia that infiltrates everything she does. My eyes hover at her panties. Just a simple black thong, but I can see the spot at the center between her thighs is wet.

"Spread your legs." My voice comes steady, soft but firm with a clear direction, and I notice her pupils dilate as she complies instantly. Her feet slide across the carpet and her thighs spread just a few inches. But it is enough; it is exactly what I wanted.

My hand rises upwards slowly but surely and I make sure that the first touch she feels is my palm against her panties. I take her most intimate place in my hand, cupping until I can feel her heat, the throb, her pulse. I can feel that wet press too. She is already so turned on, so needy, so fucking desperate.

And it makes me hunger for her even more.

"Good girl," I whisper, and she lets out a tiny, whimpering moan, and that is when I know I have her and she has me. Right where we wanted each other.

I begin to move my hand, letting my fingers stretch out between her thighs and stroke lightly against the damp fabric of her panties as my palm presses more firmly against her. A mixture of softness and pressure as my wrist lightly circles.

"Take off your bra." My voice is detached with no hint of warmth, light as a whisper. I know she has to be alert, focused to even hear me, but of course, she is and she does.

I can feel her tremble against me, her body reacting to each and every touch as her fingers glance at her spine and reach for the clasp of her bra. It takes her a moment to unhook. I'm patient ...just. I watch the front fall with a light bounce then the slow roll of her shoulders as she slips the straps off her smooth skin. Left then right... I watch everything. No detail left unsavored as her bra falls.

Her breasts are perfection, softly sculpted against her chest, her ivory white skin contrasts beautifully with the rose-pink hue of her nipples. Her nipples are hard and full, and I bet they ache to be touched and caressed.

She watches me, nervously. For a woman who lives in the spotlight and usually exudes confidence; right now, I can sense her insecurities, feel her nerves and her need to please. It is a balance; she craves submission but needs attention and affection, and I intend to give it to her.

I lean in as my chin tilts upwards. My fingers and wrist are stilling but my grip is still there against her warm pussy. I let my breath out slowly through parted lips so she feels the cool kiss of it against her skin, and I watch the goosebumps rise and her nipples become even more engorged. She trembles in my palm and I squeeze reassuringly in response.

My mouth parts wider and my tongue darts to

her nipple, just in time to make contact with the soft swell of her flesh. She gasps at the touch but I give her no relief. I only circle it slowly, watching both nipples grow harder, to the point of pain, knowing she is desperate ... needy ... willing ... and only then do I give her the first soft kiss.

My lips are soft and gentle, the lightest of touches, letting her enjoy the sensation, and then I open and draw her nipple into my mouth with a suck.

I try to tease, to put her first, but at this point, my own desire burns strong. I take a deeper suck and taste her, I let my tongue swirl round and round then flick, slow at first and then faster and faster around her nipple until her gasps became soft light moans.

She starts to rock; her body now impatient. Taking any relief she can from moving herself against my palm. I could stop her; I know that if I tell her to stop, she will, instantly. I sense that the control and power is all mine, and I like it. But I don't want her to stop. I want her to come like this for me, helplessly giving in to her own wants and desires.

I alternate my mouth from her left nipple to right and back to left. My lips grow softer with saliva as I toy and tease. The fabric of her panties grows wetter and wetter too against my palm. The material sticks as we both move in harmony. I can feel my own desire too, my own lust humming loudly between my legs, but I ignore it; I want to give her this and focus only on her.

She starts to beg. "Alexa ... please. Can I? Oh ... Please." Her voice low and gravelly and begging me is the most erotic thing I have ever heard. I don't stop to answer, just a firm nod as my teeth take her nipple and pull a little, a tiny tug of intent. Her hands drop to my shoulders where she grips me, holding on tight as she lets go.

I ride each long wave with her, supporting her body as her legs turn to jelly and she trembles and shakes.

I feel achievement and power tempered with an insatiable lust for her.

This is just the beginning and we both know it.

Fucking her like this- I have barely even started; This is a raw, needy sign of my intent for her.

Feeling her come hot and hard through the soaked fabric of her panties against my hand makes me only want more of her.

I guide her down to the sofa beside me and she

takes me by surprise. I expect a detachment but instead, she wraps herself around me, pulling me close so I can feel her tremble against my body, her racing pulse slowing as I hold her to me. Her gasps turn to pants that slow to deep breaths.

I don't speak, I just hold her like that, letting my fingers slowly trace up and down her back as she falls apart in my arms and I cherish every second.

5

Sometimes after sex—or an orgasm—it can feel awkward. A tension in the air and a question posed of *what is next?* But it doesn't work like that with Dahlia. As her body relaxes and the waves subside, she moves away from me but only to reposition herself so she can look straight at me with slightly flushed cheeks and sparkling emerald green eyes.

"I am going to shower and then we should talk, or get food or ... something." She lets her voice trail off as she makes her way out of the room and off into the bedroom. I hear her humming and then the burst of water and I try not to think too hard about the water running over her body right now and her perfect nakedness feeling that cool wetness washing away the remnants of her orgasm for me.

Instead, I distract myself. Reaching for the paperwork, I start to flip through it again. Most of it I would never do anyway. Record information, take photos, sell stories. There are some weird points that I imagine came from others pushing the rules in other ways so it had crept into the list. *You will not influence the calorie intake...* I mean, what was that all about? I wasn't about to force feed her chocolate cake, was I? Or restrict it for her. Although, I could think of lots of ways we could have fun with cake...

I feel uncomfortable about the money. I don't want to be paid for my services, but everything between us- it doesn't feel transactional. It feels real.

Dahlia is right, though. I could use the money for something useful like my coaching or competitions or something, and if I still don't feel good about it, I could just donate it or give it to Grandmama, either way, there is a solution so as not to make it into a big deal.

I pause more over the BDSM section. It is something we will need to talk more about; I will have to try and understand her needs as well as balance my own. *Dominant* is a label I can wear happily, *Domme*—perhaps not so much. But what is the difference? I suppose it is the dynamic with the other person that defines those terms, and right now Dahlia and I are right at the beginning of our sexual journey; I don't need to push it and I'm happy to see where it takes us.

She pads back into the room freshly washed and dressed, a little less relaxed but still casual in a light day dress, sandals, and damp curls pulled up high on her head so they tumble in all directions.

"We can go out for food if you want, or we can just order in for now and go out later? Unless you have other plans?"

I do have plans this afternoon but only with the pool. She catches my flicker of hesitation and misinterprets it instantly. "Or you know, another time or something."

"No, no. I would love to have lunch with you and then dinner sounds perfect too, but I have to get to the pool. I have this swim session I am supposed to do. I would skip it but my coach will bust my balls if I don't go..." I let my voice trail off as I try and think of the best way to manage it.

"Oh, that is no problem. If it is ok with you, we

can have lunch and then we can use the pool at Howard Hall. I should probably do some exercise anyway. I'll call ahead and book it out so we have privacy. It's across the city a little, but I have a driver so it won't take more time than you going to your pool. I would come to your pool but ... well, I tend to cause chaos wherever I go," she says with an apologetic shrug as she reaches for the drawer and pulls out a room service menu. "Does that work for you?"

Howard Hall. I immediately recognise the name. It is the most exclusive and expensive spa facility in the city- probably in the country.

"Yes, I mean that would be great, but I didn't bring my swimwear," I say with a doubtful voice and she grins at me wickedly as she pulls out her mobile phone.

She shrugs and her eyes glint and she seems so much more alive than I have yet seen her. "I mean, I don't see the issue with swimming nude- but okay," she says mischievously before her voice lightens to that sing-song sweetness. "Oh, hey. I need the pool at Howard Hall at 2pm booking out for like, two hours. Yes. The main pool- the one where you could do athletic stuff like swim lengths. Can you arrange a car to drive me there?

Also, I have a friend joining me. I need swimwear for her, something sporty you can actually swim in not something that just looks pretty. Get me maybe, ten options, I want a choice for her. Size..." Her eyes run over my body for a second as she pauses to assess. She doesn't ask me. I shouldn't be surprised, but it does surprise me that famous people live like this. "UK Size 12. I need all the other stuff too ..." There is a pause "I don't know, like goggles or something. Whatever people need who are swimming to actually work out, that kind of thing. Yes. Yes. Okay. Mmmm. Right, thanks hon."

She ends the call and saunters over, sliding the room service menu across to me. "I will let you look first." She smiles and I laugh.

"I work here, I know this menu better than anyone. I know what I am having. Thanks for the swim stuff, by the way. I appreciate it."

"You can order for us both then, given that you are an expert. Please, no need to thank me. They give me stuff like that for free for the chance that maybe I will be spotted in one of them and it is free publicity for them. Better that you can make actual use of them." She hands me the phone to make the room service order and then sits down opposite me.

As I dial through and ask for the best options, I see her gaze move to the legal papers that have been moved, obvious that I have been reading through, looking, thinking. The moment I hang up the phone she looks straight at me.

"I am sorry for the curveball of the contract. If I had mentioned it before you came over, I didn't think you would, but you could mention even just the fact I had offered you a contract for sexual services to the media and it could have huge consequences for me. I'm usually a good judge of character, but I have paid heavily for it in the past when I have been wrong. Do you have any questions that you want to ask me? Anything you want to talk about?"

"I guess for me, Dahlia, I don't know how to start something in this way. With contracts and rules of engagement. I mean I signed it, sure, so you know you can trust me and open up to me. So now I have done that, I would rather it just be normal between us, you know? Let things develop naturally? I get that the situation is unorthodox and it isn't like I make a habit of sleeping with famous women, so I don't have any real answers. I would just like to get to know you, spend time with you and see how it goes. I will be honest; I am not looking for anything serious in my life. I need to focus on my career, on athletics, but I like you. I am attracted to you immensely and I would like to explore that with you."

She takes each word I say and seems to digest them, letting them swirl around her head and her thoughts before she answers.

"I'm not here for long. A few more weeks, I would say. I have done this before; often the other person feels more comfortable going through each point on the contract together. This can help you to understand expectations, lines and limits, but perhaps they come from a different place. I have generally met them in the... well, different circles. It isn't every day, I find myself irresistibly drawn to the hotel bartender. For me, I am happy to explore and experiment together. I suppose we have already shown a level of compatibility," she adds with a little blush, and I smile in return.

"I have always been naturally dominant in the bedroom, but I have never explored it much further than that. Some handcuffs, a little denial, teasing, but nothing more. What kind of things do you like? I think that is something we should go through together."

She looks at me from under eyelashes so impossibly thick, I find it hard to believe they could be real, but I think that they are. Her gaze is focused on me. She is constantly assessing me; I can feel her eyes analyzing every single detail to see how I react and respond to her so she can adjust accordingly.

"I am submissive. The term is broad and can mean many things." She needs to keep her lovely graceful hands busy. I watch as she shifts and moves, reaching for the water just to pour a glass as something to do. "In the lifestyle, there are terms and roles but I don't much care for them; they draw lines where they don't need to be. There are moments when vanilla sex is what I crave, what I need, but in general… I like bondage, specifically rope play. I like to be denied, toyed, teased. I enjoy being directed, guided and controlled. Pain beyond the mild, isn't something I gain pleasure from. I can appreciate the sting of a spank, the pull of flesh as I orgasm, but I am not seeking the feeling of real pain—or marks being left on my body. There are clubs and events for the lifestyle. I like those too, but they require time to plan and a lot of paperwork for someone like me to be able to attend with my privacy observed. It gives my lawyer and manager a headache, so I save those for special occasions." She laughs, but I know it also isn't a joke.

"Did your ex like these things too?" I ask, and her eyebrows raise in question until she slots the pieces together.

"Jayden?" she asks. I nod and she smirks then pauses, weighing her words carefully. "He was into his own things." Her remark doesn't answer my question but it signals the end of the conversation, which comes just as the hotel room doorbell chimes with a ring.

We stay in the main living area to eat. I ordered an array of things. Some salads, pasta dishes and beautiful breads, meats, and cheese. I didn't know what her eating habits were and I don't want to be accused of influencing her diet, but I'm happy to see her take bits of everything and tuck in.

"I'm lucky," she says, obviously sensing I'm watching what she eats. "A high metabolism. It doesn't keep everything in shape but it certainly helps when someone puts amazing food in front of me. I don't have to starve myself to look like this and I feel grateful to my genetics for that, for sure.

Although... I am going swimming later so that will give me some balance." She giggles before twirling pasta around her fork and taking a mouthful of creamy carbonara. "Oh, this is so good. So... did I put you off?"

"Of you?" I ask with a raised eyebrow as my fork hovered midway to my lips and she nods. "I think the moment to leave was when Mr. Suit pulled out the contract. I stayed for that, so you have me a while it would seem." She laughs out loud, a full laugh that fills the room. "The way I'm feeling I doubt anything could put me off of you."

She laughs, heartily.

"Mr. Suit. That is so funny. I am going to tell him you called him that."

"I don't think he will find it amusing."

"Probably not. I've had him with me for years. I trust him. He is effective in his job for sure, but his people skills need some considerable work," she acknowledges, and I absolutely do not disagree.

We chat while we eat. It is nice just to hang out with her. Every passing minute she becomes less Dahlia Dante the super famous movie star and more just Dahlia with who I have this amazing connection and who I am dying to know more and more about.

As 2pm approaches, we take the lift down underground to the parking floor. "The hotel is very accommodating for me. If I want to pass through the front I can, but they also allow my driver to use the service entrance to come and go so we can leave when we want without the paparazzi entourage. Which, at times like this, is a real-life saver. I mean, I don't want to be doing lengths with a camera pressed up against the window. Have you ever been to Howard Hall?"

I slide into the back of the SUV. The windows are heavily tainted so I expect it to be dark but it seems to let in a regular amount of light from outside, which surprises me. The interior is huge, everything on a grand scale, and whilst it is immaculate, there is evidence that this is Dahlia's car. There is her program slotted into the leather pouch in front and her scarf draped across the center armrest. I wonder for a second how much it costs to have something like this and a driver on standby at any given moment.

"No, I have never been. I just use the local community pool when I need to get some lengths in. Generally, I prefer training in the gym, or running outdoors, but there is more chance of injury, so the closer I get to a competition the more

I switch to do my conditioning sessions in the pool to keep me at peak fitness and take any pressure off my knees and ankles."

"I never even asked. What kind of event do you do? It is track and field?" She looks at me quizzically. We call it Athletics, Americans call it track and field.

"I used to do a few different events but I found my stride with the 10k race. I like the length and the duration. It works for me."

She nods. " It seems like a long way to run. I don't know anything about sports really. I watch the Olympics and things like that occasionally, but I never follow anything."

"I will be honest... I don't watch that much sport. Like, my coach is the one who follows the other athletes in my races; he tracks their strategies and we adjust my race plan accordingly. I watch replays and study their forms for example, but that is all part of my training. I'm not a huge fan of watching team sports at all. If the track and field is on, I will watch it and the Olympics for sure. But I guess I am just more of a doer than a watcher."

"Oh, I thought you would be super like obsessed with it all!" she exclaims and I laugh.

"No, I am only obsessed with my own training and competition, no one else's."

The car starts to make its way out of the city, and I see open land and green horizons, but not for long. Howard Hall is just on the very edge of the center, making the most of the proximity whilst claiming the only green views on this side of the city before you hit suburbia. The SUV rolls silently up the long entrance drive and I watch the spa come into view. I would guess that at some point it had been an estate house that had since been remodeled to accommodate luxury clientele.

As we pull to a halt, the driver who has so far been silent, speaks to Dahlia with a soothing, soft voice. "Your bags are in the back, ma'am, I will get them for you, one moment." And he cuts the engine before silently slipping out. For a large burly guy, he moves with ease and stillness, which instantly makes me think he is ex-military. There is a subtleness to each of his actions that tells me he is way more than just a driver. And Dahlia immediately confirms my suspicions.

"Todd is my bodyguard too. Well hell, you can add a whole long list of other things he does for me too, but that is his actual title. He has worked with me for …" she pauses, thinking, just as Todd opens the back door and offers Dahlia a hand to help her out. "How long have you been helping my ass now, Todd?" she asks him and he replies instantly.

"Seven years and four months now, ma'am."

"There you go." She laughs, "My longest and most functional relationship." She smiles at him and he gives a light smile back, but I wonder what he hides behind that wall of professional politeness. Whether he feels more for her. I wouldn't blame him either if he did. She is something else.

She takes the bags from him and threads her arm through mine as we make it inside the foyer. It is surprisingly quiet. I look to Dahlia in question and she whispers to me, "I booked it all out so we wouldn't be disturbed. We have the place to ourselves other than the staff. Swim first?"

I nod and follow her lead trying to hide my shock. I wonder how much it would cost to book out something like this place for your own privacy. How you would even explain that to other clients? To cancel all the appointments? I guess she makes it more than worthwhile for them, but it seems so excessive and unnecessary. Well, to me anyway. I guess I have never experienced intrusion into my personal life.

She seems to sense my judgement.

"If I didn't, someone would make a call within five minutes. Or a sneaky cellphone video that they upload online. Then the paparazzi would descend and some would wait outside the gates, sure. I know you are thinking about the hacks that lie in wait outside the hotel hoping to catch a snap of my panties or whatever. But no, it would be women, girls, that they send into the spa area that look normal. Booking a spa. Last-minute cancellation. And you wouldn't see them, you wouldn't notice them. But she would see everything, listen to every conversation and take photo after photo on her phone, iPad, whatever. We would be none the wiser, and then an hour later when we leave, we would be splashed all over TMZ. Misquoted and lied about to get flashy headlines and fuel for the clickbait parade. *Your* life would be investigated, you would be followed and your link with me would drag you into everything. It would cost me more in legal fees proving it was all BS and getting them to take it down after the damage has already been done. So, yeah. Better this way."

She guides me to the locker rooms as she talks, and I find myself gaining more and more comprehension about what we are doing here. The risks she's taking and the difficulties she may face purely in living her life. And indeed in trying to integrate me into it. I am a tiny bit distracted though—her arm threading with mine brings a closeness, I could pinpoint all the places that we touch. My side and her hips, our thighs, our arms. Just light glances as we move, but it makes it clearer to me now, just how little contact we have had with each other and how much I want that to change.

The locker rooms are anything but rooms, rather private suites with heated floors, new fluffy towels, slippers, hair ties, an oversized shower with more hair products than my local supermarket stocks. We slip into different rooms and Dahlia hands me a bag that I empty out onto the sofa. Not sure when I would ever need to use a sofa in a locker room but it comes in handy nevertheless.

The swimsuits are all designer sportswear. All ten together must have cost more than my paycheck along with the newest release of goggles, nose clips, stopwatch. There is even a brand new Fitbit and Whoop Band, both of which I already have, and a swim specific ankle band that measures your vitals as you swim. Whoever Dahlia had spoken to had spared no expense in providing

Dahlia with the top range of swimming products and accessories.

I slip into the black Nike swimsuit. It is the same brand as I would usually wear. It fits me perfectly and feels weightlessly smooth against my skin. I tie my hair up high but don't bother with the swim cap. I fasten the band around my ankle; I am intrigued to see how accurate it will be.

Taking the goggles and the towel, I pad out to the pool. I check the measurement and it is a good length, a little longer than the local pool but narrower, not that that makes any difference when you are the only one here.

I reach the end of the tiles, my blue-painted toes curling around the edge as I look down at the crystal-clear water, my reflection rippling across the surface. I stretch my arms out high above my head, my muscles tighten, fingers lacing together, and with a soft bend of my knees I push off, and my body curves into a graceful arc. The tips of my fingers hit the cool water first but in seconds I'm in deep ... gliding across the blue mosaic floor.

Breaking the surface, I feel the cleanse of the water washing away any thoughts. Moving into the shallower end as my body moves across the water, my feet can finally touch the floor. I pause, tilting my head forwards before I flick my hair back, a glistening ray of droplets painting a rainbow in the dazzling summer sun that shine through the wall-sized French window that brings the outside in, and I continue my way forwards. Water drips from my eyelashes. I love the water.

Turning back to face the deep, my body longs to feel the weight of the water, the silence of the unknown. I dive under again. The ripples send tingles along my skin. I feel my nipples harden in the cold, my sex held in a watery caress that tingles against my intimate spots as I swim, gliding through the pool, my fingers outstretched and my hair fanning out behind me. Minutes pass and my lungs cry for fresh air; I rise up to the surface at the edge before I catch my breath then turn to repeat it over and over. I work my body, pushing myself until I find the rhythm that makes my muscles ache.

After a while, I forget where I am until I catch Dahlia in the corner of my eye. She is sitting on the edge of the pool. Her toes dance along the top of the water, skimming the surface lightly, making a soft splash. She too is in a one piece swimsuit, but unlike mine that clings to my athletic figure, her nude toned suit kisses her feminity in ways I long to.

I break from my lengths and make my way to her, pulling the goggles from my eyes and letting my hair loose just as her hands curl around the edge and she lowers herself into the water straight into my arms. She trails her fingers through my wet hair, as I guide us into shallower water, the moment my toes touches the tiled floor and I can steady myself, my hands are on her.

My palms cup her face as I draw her into me, my wet lips are hungry to kiss, and they do. Over and over. How have I waited so long to feel this? To taste her, to touch her like this. Starting at the edge of her lips, moving across, every inch I pepper in soft needy kisses. Her hands move to the straps of my suit, pulling each one so they slip from my shoulders and my small breasts are freed, and my pussy bared as the fabric falls away as she slides her hands down my thighs, meeting her toes which carry it the rest of the way.

I follow and repeat in response. Slipping the straps of her suit from her shoulders and peeling it inch by inch down her skin. I want to watch; I want to see her nakedness, but I can't stop kissing her so instead I wait for the touch. The first press of wet skin on skin. There are no barriers between us now. No fabric to show restraint; it is hard to see where I end and she begins. I feel the fullness of her breasts press against my own and I need to touch them, my kisses run down her neck and along her collarbone, the swell of her full, beautiful breasts rise just out of the water and my head dips to take her nipple lightly between my lips.

I feel her moan, it vibrates through her body. She tightens her legs around my thigh and slowly starts to rock her body against me, again and again, her slick wetness making each slide an easy glide.

With each of her movements, I feel that pressure against my sex, her thigh claiming each wanting rock along my leg, which only makes my pussy press more firmly against her leg. I take her breasts, both of them in my palms, and I cup them as I raise my head up to seek out her kisses once more.

It is not like before where I claimed her and it is not like in her contract where I take what I want. It is mutual. A climax built on mutual lust and desire for each other. Both of our bodies work in effortless harmony. We start to build together, moaning into each other's mouths. I taste her gasps as she feels the squeeze of my hands.

Water splashes as our bodies tremble, each kiss deeper and more frenzied. "Dahlia," I pant against her lips, and she responds with a soft bite. The shock sends me over the edge, the release that has been building, since the moment I met her... finally. I cling to her and feel her body mirroring mine. Waves and waves of pleasure as we ride out our orgasms.

I guide her back to the wall and pin her there. Keeping us held tight together. My body... I can't feel my toes and I am shaking so hard my muscles spasm. In every way, it is nothing special of an orgasm but in every single way, it is more than I have ever felt. The most special orgasm.

And even now my kisses don't stop. Won't stop. I can't help it. I want her taste on my tongue, on my lips, in my mouth.

"Alexa," she whispers softly against my lips, and it takes a second, a minute, but I hear her and drop slowly back down to earth.

"Sorry, did I hurt you?" I ask in a daze, unsure how tightly I held her, how hard I pushed, how needy I was with her.

"No, you didn't hurt me. But I have a feeling

6

I wait for her in the hotel lobby. We are going for dinner. Casual, nothing fancy, and she has the car primed and ready to go, but she has asked me to take a few days off, so I am currently bartering with Robbie over the bar about what it will take to have my holidays at such short notice.

The truth is, he doesn't have much choice. I am already owed a ton of days off and he can't afford to piss me off too much, but he is trying to work it in his favor. He is still talking, debating, but I give him the look as I shuffle in my all-around black dress. It neatly fits my body without being over revealing in any way. I wear it with flat shoes; heels are not for me. I am pleased I got Dahlia to drop me at home so I could change and make a little effort. I feel comfortable, a little sexy, and it is helpful that we don't have to hide our friendship so much since Dahlia has apparently intervened on my behalf.

She told me that Mr. Suit handles all that. As well as any CCTV that may have been at the pool earlier. Apparently, the hotel here has agreements so as long as we are publicly only friends only nothing will happen when it comes to my job and it won't be mentioned to me in any way. Robbie finally nods and saunters away and I feel the air change.

I know she is here the moment she arrives. But I play on it; I know she is looking at my body in this dress. I know it looks good on me. Simple, yet so tightly fitting, it shows off the body I work so hard on. I bite my lip, slowly... Exaggerated. I flick my loose hair so my neck is bared and inviting. And then, only then, I meet her gaze.

I memorize as much of her as I can from across the lobby—I've been memorizing all weekend. I see the tiny strands of hair that drape down against her neck, loosened and fallen from her bun. She is in stockings. I have visions of catching them between my teeth. But I stand still. Staring... Until my eyes flick over towards the elevator. Giving a command without saying a word.

Turning away from her, I slowly take another sip and settle the drink back at the bar. I pause then turn glance to see if she has followed my command and she has. I don't look at her again but I stand and walk like I know she is watching. My hips sway. My dress clings to my ass. Can she see a panty line? Does she wonder if I'm wearing any? My shoes click across the floor as I make my way and stand beside her as the elevator door pings open. She hovers wondering whether to go down to the car or back up to the room.

I give her no indication. I want to see if she follows my look or what she should do.

I lean back against the gold brass railing, opposite of her, just looking, making sure she sees my lust-filled eyes already undressing her, imagining peeling that dress from her... and I reach over and press the button for her suite.

I am brazen with it, my eyes sweeping downwards and back up, I smirk as I press the button. Higher and higher we rise. My heart beats fast. But I don't say a word. I don't move an inch. I just watch her. We mutually engage in a thick, hot, mental foreplay without the slightest movement outside of our wandering eyes. Not a word is spoken, but my intentions couldn't be clearer. I'm calm, put together, cleaned up on the outside. But on the inside, I'm a ravenous animal, and I've found my prey.

My mind swirls as she reaches into her pocket and pulls the silver keycard out as the *ding* rings out and the doors slide open. She steps forwards and opens her door.

This time we don't linger in the lounge area and I don't ask permission as I step towards the bedroom. Luxury. Money. Class. But I know now that I belong in her intimate world. I walk past her close enough to touch, but I don't. I flick my hair though so she gets a deep breath of my perfume. I leave my bag on a side table. I drop my jacket on a chair. My finger runs the length of a shelf as I look around. Unashamed and indiscrete in snooping. Wanting to know everything about her without asking anything.

She finds the bar, flicking the door open she lowers slowly, leaning forward, her breasts strain with a soft swing as she rocks her hips from side to side in mock contemplation. She reaches, taking out a bottle of something sparkling. She turns to me, perfectly arched eyebrows raised in question—not for permission, rather, if I would like to share. She shuts the fridge door with her heel.

She is absurdly sexy. Every movement, every micro expression, every flex of her body language. The animal inside me claws at the bars—I want to tear her apart. But I remain calm on the outside. I'm aware of my panties growing wetter, but I'm okay with that. And I respond to her eyebrow, with a single drop of my chin, a nod of affirmation, just a single lift and drop of my chin, taking a long, fluid two steps towards her.

Her fingertips twirl the wire, slowly unpeeling the foil around the top of the bottle, her palm rides up the bottle neck—a swift, tight, grip—as her hand twists. The pop is soft, the bubbles rise then simmer. She brings the bottle to her lips, rimming the top with a slow sweep of her tongue. Then her lips part, a brush of deep red lipstick marks the glass as she takes a mouthful, but as she lowers the bottle, a drop drips, runs from her lips down her chin. She catches it with her fingertip and offers it to me. No hint of a smile. Just a pure desperate lust in her face.

I move to step up into her space, and before her hand is even properly extended, I catch it in my palm, her fingers held out, my thumb pressing against her palm. I lean in, my eyes looking straight into hers and move my chin towards her finger, except I don't...

Instead, I exhale deeply, letting my guttural breath warm her collarbone, taking her by surprise as my tongue extends and the very tip drags up the soft skin of her throat, curling upwards under her chin and catching the faintest hint of champagne still left on her chin, licking all the way up and only pulling away the second my tongue touches her bottom lip... letting her watch as it disappears back in my mouth and I savor the taste.

She gasps; her breath caught as my touch takes her by surprise. She can feel me on her skin, the line I have drawn burns. I watch her body react instantly. The jolt of my touch reverberates through her. She nearly drops the bottle, I see it slipping from her fingers, much like her control. She wants me. Her green eyes drown in mine and they beg wordlessly *take me*.

I can see the submission in her once proud and defiant eyes. As the bottle begins to drop, I catch it in my hand. I'm sharp as a tack and don't miss a thing. My fingers brush against hers as I take the bottle from her. My other hand reaches up to her neck, gently stroking her throat where my tongue just was, curling around to the nape of her neck and turning her body a half turn. My other hand assists after I set the bottle on the table, and I twist her around and step up, giving her that first feel of my body against hers as I settle her against the glass, her ass pressing into me.

Only inches from the floor to ceiling 85th-floor windows, she feels the push of me, and her hands instinctively move up to the glass to stop herself—we are viewing the blacks and gold and whites of the darkened city and the flickering lights—her palms slide up along the crystal-clear glass. I want to make her feel like she is being stretched out and put on display to the city below. I feel her shivers against my lips as my lips brush against her neck, sending goosebumps down her arms. I push my body into her, pressing her forwards, knowing she will feel the cold glass against her nipples through the thin fabric of her dress. She presses against the glass, a slight push, and her ass rocks back against me, the curve of her cheeks brushing the swell of my clitoris, letting me know she feels my desire too.

My left hand slides up her ribs while my right

hand slides down from her collarbone. They meet at her breasts— full, phenomenal breasts that spill over the top of the deep red dress—just aching, begging for me. I take two handfuls, squeezing them together, kneading, letting her feel that pressure and angsty hunger exhibited by my hands.

And then my thumbs hook the top edges of her dress and pull down so slowly... so fucking slowly... so just her nipples peek out, and I press myself against her firmly, shunting her body forward so her nipples kiss the cold glass directly this time.

She lets out a low moan as her nipples feel the cold. I know she needs attention between her legs —a touch, a lick, anything. I continue to peel her dress from her skin, slowly riding that curve and discover her secret. No panties, no bra...

This Hollywood star is just a slutty girl in a red dress for me; Now she is only in stockings, and heels and the remains of the dress bunched at her hips. And she is all mine to tease, toy and play with.

Her head turns to the side and my lips capture hers. I know her lipstick leaves deep red stains against my skin and I don't care. I can feel her lust bubbling to the point where she is losing control.

I break away from the kiss and scrape my teeth

against her shoulder. Her body has been slowly bared and put on display, her dress bunched at her hips, her heels causing her ass to rise up and out, welcoming me home. I glide my hand across her breasts and squeeze a nipple, delighting in her gasp and moan.

My other hand moves, fingers searching just for the heat of her sex and her wetness. My fingers press against the fabric of the dress and touch the tip of her labia through the fabric. She tries to adjust her stance so I touch her clit, but I let her burn. She'll feel me when I'm ready. Finally she hears my voice, the lowest whisper, like a breeze, but deep. I'm sure she can hear my desire.

"Do you want me to touch you, Dahlia?"

She nods and gasps, "I need you. Please."

Her voice is weak.

That's all I want. My right hand reaches back up and settles on her throat, keeping her where I want her. With my left hand I help myself to wriggle out of my own dress.

Then I use the full, warm stroke of my fingers between her soft thighs. And I feel her wetness drip down onto my palm.

Fuck, she is so wet.

"Reach down. You may touch them. Feel my fingers against you, guide them, Dahlia."

One of her hands stays on the glass, the other snakes down, riding over her breasts, her dress, sweeping down to her pussy.

My own pussy aches for her as I watch her in the mirror-like reflection of the window.

She takes my palm with soft delicate fingers and guides my fingers with hers between her labia, coating them in seconds, she is dripping with lust. My fingers smear, touching everywhere. She feels so good. She moans and it catches in her throat, vibrating against my fingers as I hold her there.

I sway gently forward and back, her fingers slippery and delicately wrapped around mine. I can feel the pulsing heat coming from inside her, testing the limits of my restraint.

I can't wait to be inside her. I want it more than I have ever wanted anything.

The contact has been made— there is no stopping now. My fingers stroke over her clitoris before pulling back and circling, teasing, threatening to penetrate her.

She is dripping and shaking, her legs tense as she balances in her heels, the angle awkward, her ass jutting out. It is a sexy display for me and indeed for anyone looking up at the 85th floor. And that thought makes me moan. Her desperation for me is in full view as she lets out a whimpering cry. "Please ... Alexa..." she whimpers and her ass pushes back at me again. She is so open to me.

Fuck. You are mine, I think to myself. My finger gives a firm rub of her clit, a circular rub, and with each press of her clitoris, I can hear her moan. Fuck, I love it. I hold her pleasure entirely in my hands. My hands become needy in seconds. I move faster, my fingers sliding easily between her legs.

I push her legs outward, making room, and then I begin to push my fingers inside of her. I want her to feel totally opened wide and stretched for me as I push deep inside of her as far as my fingers will go.

Fuck. Her head turns and my mouth seeks hers out, and the kiss consumes us both as my fingers impale her. She is hot and hopelessly slippery as I thrust in hard and deep. I feel her adjusting around my fingers, two and then soon after, three. The angle is awkward, but I make sure my fingertips are hitting her G spot as I fuck her. She gasps and bites my lip, but I don't pause, I add a fourth finger and continue fucking her. Hard.

I'm lost in sensation when the explosion comes and bursts from deep within her. I feel it, feel her vagina tighten as she calls out loudly and her pleasure floods the back of my hand and puddles on the expensive carpet as my fingers slide out of her.

Her legs give way and suddenly it is just me and the window pane holding her up.

Fuck. I am so wet, too, with the grind of her ass against me my only relief. But it is all her. She has all of my focus and attention.

My kisses turn dirty; dirty kisses for a dirty girl. The animal bursts free from within me and the mood changes. That red dress that drew me in, caught my eye... now it's just a hindrance and something else between me and her. I lift it up and over in a flash ... her breasts bouncing freely as she stands, splayed, for all the city to see ... making me feel like I could come for her this very instant.

I drop my hand from her throat, but before she can turn, I give her a good hard slap on the ass, tanning her skin to a bright burning pink. I want to take her again. I don't care that she's barely finished coming once already. I push my hand roughly between her legs from behind again and push my four fingers straight back into her, finding her G spot immediately. She gasps and her body shakes as I begin to fuck her again hard and fast with no remorse.

She gushes for my fingers. Once. Twice. Thrice. She keeps on squirting and I keep on fucking her.

I want to orgasm. I want her to see just how wet she makes me, how hard I can come for her before I make her come again for me, so I pull from her, my fingers dripping, and I direct her until she is on her knees but to the side so we are in profile against the window. I want anyone watching to see the bob of her head as she pleasures me with her mouth.

She whimpered as my fingers slid out of her. But now she is on her knees for me and instinctively using her fingers to part my labia as her eyes close underwear thick lashes and she moans as her mouth opens to take me.

I hear my own moans escape my lips as her tongue moves in long hungry strokes taking me in desperately.

Fuck, I've never been wetter, and it turns me on like nothing else seeing her on her knees with her pretty face between my legs.

I watch her. I watch her tending to me,

caressing me, adoring me as her mouth opens and she sucks against the heat of my sex. I cry out into the room. A loud roar, and her lips and hands must feel the spasm as I let go and begin to take my pleasure from her face.

One hand tangled in her thick red hair pulls her face tight against me. Within seconds of grinding on her face, my orgasm hits me. My orgasm is long, hard and deep. It shakes me to my core and I feel as though I'm in another world where only we exist.

I come back to earth when I feel the soft lap of her tongue as she licks and licks as though to clean up every drop of my pleasure.

My orgasm comes again and again in a way it never has before.

I continue to orgasm hard and it's all for her.

My hand grips her hair again, holding her there for it all.

As I finish and allow her to pull away, I see my wetness all over her chin and lips, her make up is a mess and I like it.

I kneel down opposite her and kiss her deeply, licking and sucking the remnants of my own desire from her chin, lips, tongue. I can't get enough of her. Us. This.

And then I move to sit on the floor, spreading my legs and pulling her over to sit between them, her back against me so she faces the window again. I spread her legs with my ankles—pulling her open for the city to see her aching pussy—and reach up, putting my fingers to her mouth, she opens and sucks them obediently, no doubt they still taste of her, and when they are suitably wet I take them and press them against her throbbing, needy pussy. We stare at each other in the window as I begin to rub her clitoris.

Her arms curl back and up around my neck and her body trembles against my chest. I'm enjoying having her spread wide while I touch her and watch the reflection of us over her shoulder in the glass. And she submits entirely to my every desire. Her only answers are moans.

Her moans that get louder as my fingers start to move faster.

Her eyes are closed.

"Open your eyes. Watch yourself." I growl.

"Fuck... Fuck..." she cries as her eyes open and I watch them flit across our reflection. She watches her body opened up for me, and indeed for anyone who might care to look at this window.

I watch her too as I feel her clit swollen and

responsive under my fingers. She is so incredible to fuck. I've always enjoyed women more who let go entirely and come loudly and with abandon and she is the embodiment of that.

"You're going to come for all to see. You're going squirt for me so hard, you spray that window when you come," I instruct. "Do you understand?"

Her eyes widen, but she nods obediently, her gaze still fixed on the reflection.

I lean further around her body so I can access her better, I can't resist. I want to be inside her when she comes.

My fingers tuck down and slide easily inside of her and my palm hits her clit. She calls out and her left hand grips my thigh tightly.

My fingers begin to wildly fuck her pussy. My palm presses and bangs against her clitoris. My other hand wrapped over her shoulder and reaching down to her exposed nipple.

"Your pussy is mine," I murmur as I lick her earlobe into my mouth and suck on it for the last stretch. "You can watch yourself come now for me, baby. See how wide open you are for my hand..." My fingers fuck hard and fast and I push her over the edge again. Her whole body begins to shake.

She watches—the window acting as a mirror

and her sex reflected to us both. I pull my fingers out, focusing on just her clit in those final moments. She can't control it. Her hips buck, her thighs tense. Her body leans back, her hips push forward and her head falls back against my shoulder as she lets out a scream of pleasure. And then she explodes with my hands and mouth and body consuming her entirely.

Her squirt does indeed hit the glass and I smile to myself.

Our fucking is raw. Animalistic. Primitive.

As her orgasm subsides, grasping hands turn to tenderness, pinches turn to softness. I hold her as she falls back against me and I bury my face in her wild hair, our breathing synced as we bask in the endless city lights.

She is beautiful and delicate again as she folds into my arms and I kiss her neck so very softly.

As raw as our passion is, and whatever the future of us involves, I know in that moment, I'll have infinite tenderness for her.

7

Our failed dinner turns into room service in her suite. The glass which earlier marked our stage is now our screen as we sit on the carpet and eat. I have never seen the city like this, from up so high, and been able to really appreciate it in a different way.

The lights of the traffic move in and out of the central area. A slow stream of yellows and reds. They all begin to blur so slow dots became fast lines of movement. But it isn't the ground that catches my attention the most; it's the buildings around us.

Years ago, I had taken a trip to Paris over the holiday season. It had been for some competition;

I forget the details now, but I had decided to extend my stay to be there for New Year's Eve. The night itself had been unremarkable and I had learned a hard lesson at a young age—special nights are often only special because of the company you are with, and whilst there was something magical about watching the Eiffel Tower lit up at the stroke of midnight, it was certainly more magical for the people around me who were celebrating with someone else. I took the metro back to my cheap hotel out of the center of the city but the line was slow. What should have taken me twenty minutes turned into nearly an hour ride of stop-start traffic, people cramming to make it to a party or home.

The line I needed was the overground train and I remember that journey as if it were only yesterday. Staring out of the window with wide eyes as city lights glistened in the condensation that ran down the glass. I looked up at the balconies around me, Juliet doors flung open, and the sounds of laughter, cheers, music, and life echoed around. Glimpses of friends, couples, families, and children welcoming in the new year. I caught eyes with a beautiful brunette on a balcony, she was smoking, twirling the cigarette through her fingers as only the French can, her full lips slightly parted. Her gaze lingered, as did mine and I wondered her story. Why she was alone that night. Whether she was happy or sad.

And then my train moved on and she was gone. Nothing more than a glance.

Now as I look out of the 85th floor window, naked beneath the thick white robe, I wonder how I would look if someone caught my gaze. If for a moment they saw me sitting staring out of the glass. Would they think I was rich? Imagine I had a wealthy husband? Do I look happy? Do I have that just fucked look?

I'm not sure, but whatever someone could imagine, they could surely never guess the truth.

Dahlia Dante, the movie star, settles beside me in a matching hotel robe, her body naturally aligning with my own. She is smaller than me, more petite in every way. Her face is for the first time free of make up and her hair is tied up casually. She looks younger and if it is possible, even more beautiful. She giggles as she feeds me strawberries and I laugh as she drips cream down my chest. We chat and share a tenderness that I never imagined. So many barriers have dropped between us, it is like the wall that we didn't know was there has been torn down and now all I can see is the other side, and it is beautiful. I wonder how often Dahlia lets her guard down, how much she has ever really known the freedom to be herself. She offers me a closeness and intimacy I haven't expected- that I have never really had with anyone- and when she asks me about my family, I falter. Words stick in my throat and she sees this and chooses to fill the silence.

"My daddy was a real southern man. He had money, old American money if that even means anything to anyone really, but it sure meant something to him. But he squandered it. Had no talent, no eye for investment, no work ethic or purpose. Every year the pot went down and down. My mom, she didn't marry a Dante to have to work. No, Ma'am, marrying a man like that was work enough. Then I was born and I became the meal ticket. I was talented. Do you know how many times I heard that as a kid? I was gifted. I was special. To everyone and anyone that would listen. *You know Dahlia Dante... Yeah, Bob Dante's girl. She is a gifted girl alright.*"

A darkness passes over Dahlia's face as she reaches for the wine. She doesn't bother with a glass, instead taking a long deep drink straight from the bottle. "How talented is any girl at four, you know? But you say something enough and people believe it. Then before long, you believe it. Those kids club shows ruined so many children. You don't need to look further than the group I was with to see how much it fucked them up, but for me, it saved me from the truth that I was not gifted. I wasn't special. I was just a pretty enough southern girl with a pushy mom and a good bit of luck. But when that truth hit me, when I actually realized I wasn't anything other than ordinary... The spiral came fast and hard. Except you can't spiral if you're a star because special people don't spiral." She laughs drily at the irony as she takes another deep drink.

"That is when I found my release. By accident. With a man. And if you haven't already noticed, whatever the official line is, I am not actually that interested in men period. He was a pretty good guy; he caught my attention for longer than a minute and I was way, way, *way* back in my closet then. Mentally, not just publicly. Anyway, he told me that he liked to be dominant in the bedroom and I thought, well, that could work for me, maybe if I don't need to do much, he will enjoy it more and it will last a little longer kind of thing. But something happened. The first time I felt the rope around my wrists, it was like my heart calmed. My head just stopped thinking. A feeling of peace descended and I could let go. It wasn't about me, I had no control, I could not change anything, or fix anything or fuck anything up. I could finally accept the fact that for that moment I wasn't special. I wasn't talented. I was just Dahlia fucking Dante."

She tips the bottle towards me in a mock cheers before she takes a final deep slug. I watch the last few drops drip and that's when I realize that she has finished the whole thing. Not that I care. She can drink as much or as little as she likes and it doesn't make a difference to me. I just don't want her to regret opening up. I don't want her to have any doubts tomorrow as to whether she is doing the right thing. So, I do the only thing I can think of to give her that reassurance and to show her that she can trust me and put her faith in me.

I take the bottle from her hand and I move to straddle her. My robe falls open as my knees rest on either side of her hips. My hands reach down and pull the tie around her waist until her own robe falls open to display her beautiful naked body. She lies back, her eyes wide, watching and waiting to see where I will guide her and take us. My gaze flicks from her hands to the chair.

"I want you to reach up and take the leg in your hands. I want you to grip it tightly. I am not going to tie you, but I don't want you to let go, Dahlia. No matter what I do..." I pause and my hips start to rock, my clitoris pressing lightly against her pubic mound. "No matter how much you want to..." My palms drop to her breasts and I take them, her flesh filling up my hands, and I push them up and together. "No matter how desperate you are ..." My fingers and thumbs clinch together and pinch her nipples. Starting first with a light circle, but I increase the pressure every few seconds. "You don't let go. Do you understand me?"

Even if she hadn't told me what being dominated did for her, I can see it right now in her eyes. I watch as her body calms, her mind switching off so she can forget all of her pressures and worries and just live and be in the moment. She gives me that trust, she offers me the total ability to control her, dominate her, own her body and cleanse her mind. And I take it. I want it. Fuck, I think I need it.

This time it's about me, as the dominant one you have to make the decisions. You have to read the situation, and whilst a submissive person is under your control, they hold the power. If you go too hard, too far, too selfish, too giving—you lose their trust in you.

I had focused my entire efforts on Dahlia and in the process enjoyed myself over and over again, but right now, now, I need to take. To have.

I drop my hips and spread my knees. I find that perfect spot to grind myself against her. I'm not gentle. As my hands drop again to cling to her breasts, my legs move to tangle around her, adjusting until I can move as I need. I am so very wet that as I grind against her I slide so easily. My sex slides against her body. She calls out and I hear myself moan. Loud. I can feel her under me, the memory of her taste flooding my mouth, and I lose all control.

I feel my fingertips knead into her flesh, my pelvis pressing hard against her, moving faster with a long deep drop of my hips. I feel every inch of that grind and it only makes me hungry for more. My eyes lock with hers, moans escaping her full, sexy lips. Her fingers are white as she grips the chair so tight and I watch her breasts shift back and forth as I rock against her.

She has turned me into an animal. Every inch

of her is total perfection. My hunger is only growing and growing the more I feast on her.

My climax is hard, fast, and full of rawness. I collapse beside her, legs tangled with hers, as I breathlessly tremble on the floor.

8

I wake up Tuesday in Dahlia's bed aching yet feeling so fucking good. I can't remember the last time I felt like that. I have to head out of the city to Grandmama's to pick up my clothes—not that I need them as I am taking some time off work.

I should be worrying about training. About the race coming up. About keeping my head straight, but I can't do it. I'm floating. High. High on laughter and sex and I don't want to face reality.

I stand slowly and shake out my hair and seek out a mirror. My lips are still swollen, my eyes are hazy—I look like I have just been thoroughly fucked. And I have. I take the champagne from the table with a smirk as I meander through to the bathroom and run the bathwater. I don't look back. But she knows the invitation is open.

She sits just out of sight on the edge of the bed, dialing the front desk. She glances over and just barely sees me in the mirror as my toes enter the warm water. With a quick, inaudible order I see her drop the receiver, grab a glass and head towards the bathroom as well.

I let my body sink into the hot bubbles. My body aches, but it's a good ache. The kind where you've been touched ...tasted ...enjoyed. The stream rises from my limbs as I take my legs out of the water. I reach for the soap, it is the expensive kind, my hands trail up and down my legs, knees bending so I can wash from my ankle straight to the tops of my thighs. My palms knead supple flesh with a slow, sensual rhythm.

She watches it all while leaning against the doorway. Standing stark naked, proud and confident in her physique, her beautiful red hair in long wild curls, skimming her nipples. She sips the golden bubbly and sees the soothe in my face as I feel the effects of the hot water against my sore muscles. Taking another swig, she smirks at me and swallows, slowly making her way to the side of the tub.

I drape my legs over either side. The cool porcelain feels nice against my hot skin. Most of my body hides under the water, obscured by iridescent bubbles. My breasts break the surface, my nipples are soft, the pink is rosy and light against my paleness. My hair is wet around my shoulders. I glance up at her. I watch her make her way over, her confidence, her sexiness... fuck, it captures me. And I murmur softly, "I think you should share the champagne."

She sits on the edge of the tub, her torso twisting around towards me, holding her glass out casually. "Mind topping me up?" she says, a delightfully mischievous grin stretched out on her mouth. Her other hand dips into the water and two fingertips brush against my leg, high up my thigh where my leg meets my hip.

She can see the bottle at the side of the tub where I placed it when I came in. We're playing a game. I keep my breath even as her fingers trace up my thigh. I lean forwards, my breasts rising out of the water, but I keep my legs still hooked and open wide. I reach down for the bottle, bringing it with me as I rest back in the tub. I keep my eyes on her as I lean back, my head resting on the lip of the bath edge, and I thrust my hips upwards, the water runs off my body. And then I pour champagne all over my stomach, my breasts, my pussy, until the bottle is drained.

"Take a taste."

Her whole body is given pause, and she stares. I don't think she realizes she is staring. It is so irregular for her to lose her cool, get flustered, but I can see it on her face; I've done it. She watches as the champagne flows off my body, but particularly the way it bubbles and gleams as it slides down between the folds of my pussy.

Then her head turns to look at my face, the cheeky expression I'm wearing, and the pure, dumbfounded shock on her face is replaced with a devilish smile of her own. Suddenly, she dips down, her hands moving to both sides of the tub edge, and the flat of her tongue runs down my belly, over my navel, and straight between my legs —tasting first the champagne and then my taste she finds on the tip of her tongue. Her tongue feels familiar to me now and I relax into the long slow hungry strokes of it.

I watch as she explores my body, I see the swirl of her tongue, the graze of teeth, and the press of her lips. The tip of her tongue dances along my folds. I wonder how I taste to her. I relax a little into the position, my shoulders sliding down the bath, my breasts half in, half out. Hardening nipples peeking through the bubbles. My vulva remains offered to her.

It starts with very soft kisses and she is sucking my delicate folds into her mouth. I can feel my wetness at the touch of her warm tongue. She knows I am deeply aroused. An attentive lover, she notices my legs may begin to tire, so with her left hand she curls her forearm between my legs and underneath me, her palm against the small of my back, my pussy just an inch away from her bicep— holding me up from between my legs—but she lifts higher and helps herself to more of what I have to offer. She too begins to feel the flush of arousal. I can see it in her eyes and in her body as she now leans along the side of the tub.

My hands grip the side of the tub. The soft kisses, watching her make out with my needy pussy... fuck, she is delicious. Her tongue laps at me ...and I can see my wetness on the tip of it. I let out a moan that is softer and more feminine than I imagined, light and breathless. I can't tell you how good it feels. How much I love it. "Don't stop. My clit... Yes... Lower... There... Yes ..."

I'm not shy in what I want from her and she obeys immediately. Her every desire is to please me.

I can tell she loves to hear me ask for what I want. Sometimes she obliges, sometimes she teases, but no matter what, my need is closely attended with affection and care. Her tongue exploring every crevice, every delicate sliver of skin, every sensitive spot.

She reaches her hand between my legs, dipping her fingers inside me, coating them in wetness, then bringing them up to my mouth.

She offers them to me.

"Taste for yourself," she whispers delicately.

I moan loudly at the decadence of this moment. I'm writhing, water splashing as I can barely contain myself. Sweat shines on my skin. My dark devoted eyes meet hers as I grip the tub tight and lean forwards. My suck is explicit, deep, my head bobbing and my lips smacking to make that loud sucking noise.

She can feel the masterwork of my tongue, specifically as it glides in circles around her finger mimicking the way I hungrily taste and tease her pussy. I can see she wants more, and she lays parallel with the tub, dining on me and relishing in all of the sweet reaction, she slides her thigh up onto the side of the tub, stretching her body out, and letting her pussy rest, a beckoning call, as she goes back to eating me, licking me, adoring me.

"Do you want me to taste you whilst you lick me?" I ask breathlessly.

"Last time was rushed… now you could spend a bit of time … if you like," she says as every third or fourth word is interrupted by a kiss.

I unhook my legs and let go of the tub. My body falls with a soft splash, pulled from her tongue's reach. Hot water caresses my sex, runs through my hair, over my face. I close my eyes and feel my pulse in my head. Racing. Wanting. And then I rise out of the tub. I don't pause or hesitate. My hands are on her shoulders pushing her back onto the tiled floor. My legs straddle at her shoulders as my wet body soaks her too. My clit is throbbing with need and I don't pause, my hips drop and I slide myself down onto her face as my wet hands reach between her legs.

I've taken her by surprise again. She's surprised but enthusiastic as her mouth goes to work on me.

I feel her tongue push inside of me and I grind down and moan.

My fingers begin to stroke lightly back and forth through her folds enjoying her wetness. I wonder for a moment if she is always this wet. Her moaning increases against my clit with a deep vibration.

Her knees are raised and my left hand reaches around to grab her ass firmly while my right hand continues to tease her with pleasure. Meanwhile, I'm bouncing, rocking and riding her tongue.

My wet fingers slide effortlessly, giving her lots of pressure, playing up and down against her clit, matching the pace of my hips as they fuck her face.

She doesn't resist—the opposite, in fact. The harder I grind against her face, the more she pushes her face into my dripping sex. Her tongue fucks me with abandon as I press down against her face and I sit up in enjoyment. She delivers a long, thick swipe up between my labia, then she keeps going, and her tongue laps against my anus. Her tongue teases for a second and circles before pressing hard and pushing inside my ass.

I feel every nerve ending come alive.

My right hand suddenly stops working. "I'm sorry but I need..." I moan as I rise upwards. My thighs tighten around her head, my hips dipping and rising as I use her lips, chin, tongue, nose, mouth, all of her to please me. Faster, harder. "Don't you dare stop!" I cry as my body is totally lost.

She gasps as her arms loop up and curl backward over my thighs. Her hands stretch out and grab my ass. She spreads my cheeks out before delivering two slaps. First, the right cheek, then the left. Almost before I can register the sharp pain, she spreads me nice and wide and licks me, her tongue flicks against me before turning her head to bite my ass cheek hard enough to leave teeth marks.

She then drops her head and assists in my needy grind, firming up her tongue and letting me make sure to feel everything as my pussy slides up and down her face. Sometimes she traps my clit between her lips and lets me feel the pressure.

"Yes ... yes .... fuck yes. I'm there. I'm so there." But her pussy. I need her. I want her. My hands stretch forwards, nails scraping up her thigh as my mouth hunts for her sweetness, my tongue slipping between her lips so she can feel my moans and screams. God, it's so good. "Baby, you make me so wet. So needy. I can't stop," I moan out against her.

I can't move much, I'm too far gone, but I breathe against her pussy, letting her feel my moans, pants, and gasps as I lose control and submit to her expert tongue. My knees slide wide. My pussy pressed against her face. The pressure on my clit is the most delicious sensation, and as I feel her finger push deep inside my anus, my orgasm floods through me like a tsunami taking everything in its path.

Her feet come together, her legs forming a diamond for leverage, and she thrust upwards, giving me all her pussy as I come.

The second I start to gain control, I remember I am lying on top of her and raise myself a little so she can catch her breath. But she holds my ass tightly to her and her finger is still deep inside me. She spreads my pussy with her mouth and her tongue keeps lapping gently at me.

It's her turn. I start to lick her, properly, hungrily, giving her the attention she deserves.

I am pushing through, my clit is so sensitive, it's become so hard. But I channel it. I use it to lick her harder. She pushed me to my limits, claiming all of me. Making me hers as I make her mine.

My fingers join the efforts of my tongue and tease both her vagina and her anus. I continue to lick and suck her clitoris as my own finger pushes carefully inside her tight asshole. I her her call out and feel her pull me in tighter, and it turns me on more and more as we purr and rock against and inside each other.

I push deeper inside her as she relaxes into it and I feel her deep inside my own ass.

We climax in near synchrony. There is no end and no beginning to us. Just a circle of never-ending pleasure.

~

The second attempt I make that day to get ready, I do so with no champagne, less flirting, and much more alone. I see my crumpled clothes scattered around the penthouse, and it's not like I could wear last night's outfit anyway to see my Grandmama so I have to go begging.

"Erm, Dahlia, do you think I could borrow something of yours to wear?" I ask nervously, feeling like I am being cheeky.

She is laid across the couch idly thumbing through a magazine. She is dressed in cute pants and a fitted tee. It is effortless the way she looks so good in absolutely anything.

"No, because my clothes won't fit you or suit you, but if you check the wardrobe, you will find some things your size and style. Also underwear, socks, shoes etc. They are yours, I had them picked up for you, so take whatever you want. We can order more if you need them, anything you want or need- it is just the basics to make things a little easier," she says everything so casually, but for me, it is a big deal. Like shopping but without leaving the house.

I dash back through in my towel to the bedroom and pull open the huge fitted wardrobe. It is obvious that the right side is for Dahlia. It is overspilling with outfits of all colors, shapes, and sizes, but then on the left is a tidy little section just for me.

It is all branded, expensive sportswear, and whoever ordered it knew perfectly my size, shape, and style. I pull out the drawers and find perfectly pressed panties, matched and folded socks, sports bras and crop tops. The next draw holds a little more ...well. *Lingerie* is the polite word for them, but as I pull a pair of black lace panties out, I can see the crotchless center that runs straight through the middle.

"I can get us anything like that, that you want. Outfits, toys, games. It isn't an issue. Just write a list and it will be in the wardrobe before you get back. If you want?"

I jump a little; I hadn't heard her behind me. But then I relax and place the panties back in the drawer.

"Why don't you write one, whilst I am gone. Think of the things you like, you want. what you have tried, haven't tried and then we can..." I pause as I think of the word and I feel my aching sex pulse at the thought. "Experiment," I finish.

"I can do that," Dahlia says in a light, breathless whisper.

"Good girl."

9

Her driver takes me out of the city but not all the way. Instead, I decide to run the rest. I need it, my body needs it, and my coach will kill me if I don't get some distance running in. It gives me some time to go through my thoughts and feelings.

Dahlia Dante. Already the images of her that I had have begun to fade. I don't put the real her together with the superstar I have seen on the TV and in magazines. She is not that person. She isn't who people think she is at all, and for that, I feel so lucky that I get to have the real her.

I have to rein in my feelings though which I can feel rapidly getting out of hand. That in itself is strange for me. I feel overwhelmed with tenderness for her and as I think back to past lovers, I realise it is my first time feeling anything like this.

These feelings have to calm down though.

This is only a short-term thing with Dahlia. For sure, she will leave the city within a couple of weeks. And yes, there is the possibility that she will return, but there would be no guarantee things would pick up again between us. It isn't just about the the short term nature of things. I mean, I have signed a contract, and taken money for my services for goodness' sake! I shouldn't get ahead of myself about what this is. It is sex. It is about enjoying each other right now, at the moment, and then moving on. I shouldn't waste my time thinking about anything else; I have to put a stop to my feelings that go past that point.

But they are already bubbling under the surface. She hasn't just shared her body and began to reveal her fantasies. She has let down her walls and has given me a glimpse of the real Dahlia. Her childhood, her fears, her insecurities.

I run harder and harder. Mind over body, mind over heart. It is early days and we have spent most of them having sex which obviously confuses things but I just know the feelings for her are real and have the potential to grow. The fact that I've covered 4km already and haven't stopped the inner Dahlia monologue is testimony to that.

I see the suburbs change into familiar territory. My entire childhood could be summed up on these streets. That is the house where at 15 I kissed a girl called Sophie on the sofa in her living room, and even though I said it wasn't, it had been my first kiss. Next street, my first ride on a bike without stabilizers. The third house on the left is where my closest middle school friend lived but we barely spoke after we went to different high schools. The Park ...oof, the hours I had spent in there running. Nearly every day from my early teens I had run those laps. Round and round; I could do it with my eyes closed. I still could.

I take the left turn and head in to the park. I don't need to but I'm feeling nostalgic. Even the smell of the trees is familiar, like home. I know I can slow off but I don't. I run harder and harder, covering the oval in perhaps one of my quickest times.

It is pretty much empty. It usually is. It isn't a particularly pretty park and others in the area have more for kids to do. It got more popular in January with the new-year-resolution joggers and you might see the odd yoga enthusiast in the summer, but it is mainly a place teenagers hang out in the evening. Even when I had been a teen, there had been petitions to add gates to dissuade the youths at antisocial hours... But then where would they go? And on the back of that question, the unspoken agreement was out of sight, out of mind, and as long as they kept to themselves people generally looked the other way.

Mr. Blakely had been allocated the park pick-up and clean route. Every morning at 6 am he started collecting the bottles and remnants from the night before. I always knew I was early if I got to the park before Mr. Blakely, and he would give me a smile and a wave as I passed him before humming through his picking and binning.

I wouldn't see him now though. He had retired a few years ago and since then there had been no regular council worker allocated, which meant things were a little less loved and taken care of. It didn't make much difference to me the path was still the path and the distance the same, but it was always a shame to see it a little less loved.

I run round twice and contemplate a third but my calves are on fire and sweat drips from me so I head home. Well, not to my home but to what feels like home.

The back door is open and the smells of pie are filling up the kitchen. Condensation runs down the panes as pots boil and crusts bubble and bake.

"I saw you in the park, felt like a memory watching you go round. I laid out a towel and some clothes, go shower and change," Grandmama coos, and I smile to myself as I peel my new and ridiculously expensive running shoes from my feet and make my way upstairs.

Old-fashioned is not really her style though nothing seems to have changed that much in the twenty-odd years I have lived here. No clutter is the number one rule. Everything has a place and if it doesn't have a place, it doesn't belong and that is that. There are no terrible floral prints or frilly lace. The furniture is old but the good kind of old that looks classic but sturdy. The bathroom has seen a slight upgrade in my teenage years with the acquisition of a shower, which at the time had felt like a huge deal for my post-run routine.

I strip off and walk straight into the icy cold water. My muscles scream and my heart hammers and then the soothing comes. I stand there a few minutes and just let the water pound at my skin. It feels good, like an unknotting. I smile as I catch sight of my favorite shampoo and conditioner still on the shelf. Restocked and ready for whenever I need them.

It takes longer than normal, but I give my body a long, slow clean. I run the razor over just lathered skin before toweling off and slipping into perfectly pressed clothes and warm socks. I pad down the stairs with my damp hair loose, pulling up a chair at the kitchen table.

"I made us some meat and potato pie and then apple crumble for after. I know it is a little early for the big winter dinners, but I really fancied some. I wasn't sure about your eating plan at the moment so I did extra veggies and meat just in case you need them rather than too many carbs."

I smile. "Thanks, Grandmama. I'm not shredding right now so everything sounds great. Thanks for the clothes." I nod towards the freshly pressed pile. "But I'm not working this week so you get a week off next week from ironing." I grin before taking a sip of the tea she had just placed in front of me.

"Oh, I thought your race was in a couple of weeks," she says, confused, as she heads over to the calendar.

"No, it is, it is. I am just taking some time. Training, a break from work. Hanging out with some friends."

I feel her gaze before I caught it. Looking over her glasses, she half-turns to look at me from the calendar.

"Friends plural. Or friend singular?" she asks as I turn a light shade of pink. "Oh, that color tells me it is singular. Well. Tell me about them, they must be someone special if they have you taking time off work."

She takes a seat beside me, and although I know I have her full attention, her eyes flick to the oven, pots, and pans behind me. It is an instinct, always aware of what is going on.

"Well, *they* are a *she* for starters." For some families, this may be a bigger talk, a greater reveal, especially with a grandparent. But not for me and mine. She has always been ahead of the curve, trendy before the trend with just a general feeling of right and wrong and acting on those without taking many directions from religion, politics, or other misguided notions.

Maybe if life had been different for her, she would have felt differently about the path her only grandchild took. But I often forget that she too lost more than someone should ever have to lose, a child, her only son, and I think that tilted her world axis to see much more than judging someone based on sexual orientation.

The benefit of being raised by your grandparents is that they had done it once and learned from their own mistakes. Some parents can do that with a second or third child, but usually, the age gap doesn't offer much in the terms of retrospect.

For me, they had seen how some of their actions had shaped the man my father became. The good they worked hard to ingrain in me, and the bad...well, they ditched those habits. They didn't make me into a perfect human, not by a long shot, but they did manage to create a nearly perfect home life. There was a balance, love, listening, respect, sharing, caring, and compassion.

I miss my parents. I grieve for them. But if I look at the life my grandparents gave me, I am grateful.

"Okay, well, tell me about her."

I pull a face. "Actually, this will sound crazy, but I'm not really allowed to tell you about her. I signed a contract ..."

I watch her head tilt and her eyes look me over

to see if I'm joking with her only for my serious stance to tell her I am not.

"Okay. Well, let us just pretend that I understand what that means for a moment and move on without the details. Do you like her?"

I am hesitant to answer that question. "Yes, I like her. I really like her, but it isn't a simple situation. Like I said, I can't even really talk about her but even if I could I would only say that we don't just live in different worlds, we are on totally different orbits. So, I think it is probably just a short-term thing where I should just appreciate it for what it is and how it feels right now."

"Let me tell you something, Alexa. Your dad used to go on and on about this girl in his class. From being about eleven I would say. Silly things, 'Did you know that butterflies have six legs? Jen told me today. Hey Mama, did you know that snakes can't move backward. Jen showed me at lunch how they move and it is impossible, how cool is that?' Then he got older, and he got this little pink tinge to his cheeks when he would say, 'Oh, Jen told me about this movie coming out, do you mind if I go?' Young love doesn't play by these silly dating rules and five-year plans and should you call back first." She pauses, looking at me but not really seeing, just caught in a memory.

"About thirty years ago, your father turned up at my door in one hell of a mess. Me and your grandpop were fraught with worry. Pounding on the door he was, and I thought for sure something bad had happened. I opened that door and he had never looked so disheveled. His hair was a mess, eyes wide and scared but excited. 'Mama,' he said to me softly, his voice so quiet I could barely hear him, 'Jen is going to have a baby, Mama.' Twenty-two, barely stepped out of college they had. But he loved your mom, he loved her from the day she told him about legs and snakes and all the other things he used to tell me at a hundred miles an hour after school. So, I don't know what you think about relationships, Alexa. I don't know whether me and your grandpop taught you well enough, we were old, love for us was about sharing what we had built over sixty years, not about butterflies anymore, but you should learn it from your mom and dad. Always go for what feels right now, because now ... that is all any of us ever have."

I pause, think about replying, about asking more. But I don't need to, it has all been said. I know that it is still hard for Grandmama to talk about my father; I know that she misses him far more than I ever could. To me, he represents another life, but not a person. Not a love I can remember. So, to hear her speak of him, of my mom... It means a lot to me.

We have lunch and we chat about normal things. Nothing more is said about Dahlia, but as I leave her home later that afternoon with my freshly ironed clothes and half an apple crumble wrapped in foil, she calls me from the door.

"Live for the moment, Alexa my darling, I promise you; it will always work out if you live like that."

I nod and blow a kiss as I meander away, and as if on cue, the moment I turn the bend, Dahlia's driver is sitting there waiting for me. I don't ask the how or the why. I just get in the SUV and seize the moment.

10

She begins to shuffle. I imagine her ankles are burning as the thick rope chafes against her skin. The knots on either ankle are tightly pressing against the bone and will not let up in pressure as on the opposite side of them lies the metal bar that runs horizontally between her legs.

She is pried open, nowhere to go, her knees bend back towards her breasts and her wrists attached with a second and third piece of rope, connected to metal loops at the ends of the bar. Her fingertips and freshly painted nails can merely tickle the skin of her ankles and feet, but as she lays on her back, her range of movement is greatly constricted.

At this moment, she knows I am back in the room. She heard the door open and close behind her— out of her range of view—and the slow, methodical footsteps that follow.

She has been a good girl. Ordering what she wants. What she likes. And now I have a range of things to test and try and learn at my fingertips. But first I needed to see her like this. She gave me a quick tuition on knots and then as I tied her, I kept her blindfolded. I was slow and methodical, not letting my mind take in the sight of her. I just focused on one knot at a time.

Then I left, going to the bar to pour myself a drink so I could compose myself, prepare and detach so I could see her like this with fresh eyes.

She slowly moves her limbs, testing at her restraints to see how much give she can have and how much she can move, and the truth is it's not much. Her legs are spread wide and her neatly waxed vulva is obscenely open, inviting me to look, taste, touch, fuck her. Her breasts heave with each long deep breath, and I can wait no longer.

I approach her quietly. She is lying on the floor, tied, vulnerable, ripe for the taking. The room is darkened so that it shows everything dimly. Her senses are awakened. The darkness means she can hear each movement more clearly, feel the air change as I approach. The first touch comes against her lips as her mouth is opened, her tongue flicks so she can taste my skin. And just that touch, that taste, I can tell it arouses her. I watch as her nipples harden and I feel a bolt of desire between my legs, both of us wanting more.

Her lips bend under my touch. My index finger draws a circle around the contours of her lips before sliding inside her mouth and pressing against her tongue, coaxing her to show me how she sucks. And I know she can. "Show me," I whisper.

Her lips close around my finger and her tongue swirls. Her head rises up as far as she can reach so she can bob her head back and forth to give me nice, deep, lingering sucks. Her eyes are wide and needy.

I pull my finger from her mouth sooner than she might expect, pushing against her cheek so she doesn't have a moment to close her lips, which leaves a drop of saliva on the tip of my finger. The backs of three fingers glide down the length of her neck, her collarbone, her sternum, then the gentle curve of her breast until she feels a wet push against her nipple, just the very tip. It hardens in an instant but doesn't get the satisfaction of a pinch.

She lets out a light whimpering moan and she hears the bar click as her body tenses with want, her thighs instinctively trying to close together. But she can't. So, she is left there, bare, to ache. She flexes, having no control of her wetness that drips from her exposed vulva and runs down over her anus.

My finger with just a hint of wetness left moves to her other nipple. There is a cold touch, then nothing. I let a few seconds pass and then she actually gets the pinch she desperately craves. It's slow but it's tight, and the soft skin of her breast stretches taut as I pull her nipple away from her body, then I lean down and run the tip of my tongue across her top lip then the bottom.

Her tiny moan vibrates against my tongue as I lick, the moment she feels that touch she reaches with her mouth, opening, and sucking on my tongue. My pull on her nipple is hard, her gasp caught by my lips as she feels that sharp shock of pain.

Her vulva is leaking wetness and I know she

can feel it. Warm, wet trails of her desire flow out of her and ride the contours of her lips before they sink down in between the crevice of her ass. As she rocks back and forth, her ass lifts and then I know she must feel the wetness collecting beneath her.

"You're such a dirty girl, aren't you?" my voice murmurs against her soft lips and my chin brushes against her cheek as I move to her earlobe. Both hands stretching down, taking handfuls of her breasts, harder now. Full grabs. Toying with her.

Each rough touch makes her body only want more and more. I can feel her nipples pressed against my palms as I squeeze hard. "Fuck, I want you," I groan into her ear. And her pussy shows how she reacts to my claim. Her body rocking with a need to have just any touch against her most sensitive part. Desperate to feel me against her, inside her.

"Please," she begs softly with a whimpering moan.

My hands knead her firm breasts, squeezing them fluidly but roughly. Leaving them and stretching forward, my fingers leading the way, pressing against her belly, eventually raking over her hip bones and then pressing to her inner thighs on the stretched tendon on either side. I know she can feel herself open further for me.

Then she can feel something else. The light touch of my inner thigh as it rests against her cheek, the underside of my vulva skimming against her lips. "Show me what you love."

Her lips fall open and her head tilts back. Her tongue chases through my folds, lapping up against me before she takes a long exhale than a suck inward into her mouth. She sucks on me, slowly but with a loud need, her ass tilts up, her pussy angled towards me, and she flexes, again and again. She wants me so badly and it is the biggest turn on I can imagine.

"Fuck..." she moans against me as she sucks and licks harder. Faster. Showing me with her mouth how much she needs me to touch her. Begging with her lips as she pleasures me over and over again.

One knee bends as I kneel on the other, dipping myself against her mouth and letting her have me. I dip my hips like I'm testing her out, letting her practice. Perfecting her technique. *Impress me,* my body is telling her, and she steps up to the challenge.

But my hands show her my satisfaction and let

her know how I'm impressed with her,. My fingers span outwards in star patterns touching her between her legs. My hands dance over her teasingly. My index fingers skim along her labia, pulling them open so she feels her most vulnerable to me.

"Fuck." I can't help but think she's so very beautiful when she's this slutty for me. More. I want more.

She tilts her head back further, so her crown rests on the floor. Her throat stretched out. And she keeps licking me as though she is starving and the taste of me is the only thing that will sate her hunger.

My fingers pinch her folds together, rubbing them against each other; I'm teasing her and I like it.

Before pulling away from her, my finger gives the quickest of swipes against her clit ...but hard. So, she feels it.

She moans loudly.

I stand and walk around her positioning myself between her legs.

"Jesus," she moans as I watch her body. "Fuck, I need more," she pleads and I can't resist her.

My fingers return to her body, along with my

mouth. I pull her open again and begin to lick her with long and slow strokes from her anus, up to her clitoris, pausing occasionally to push my tongue inside her as far as is possible to go.

"I can't take it. I need you. I need to feel you in me. Fuck me. Please fuck me," she begs with a wanton desperation in her voice.

"So, it's my fingers you want? Inside you? Is that what you want? What do you deserve?" I respond as I tap my fingers against her opening as I tease her. "Like this?" And I push my long fingers against her, as though I'm going to enter her, and then I stop and she cries out at the interruption.

"No." I step back for a second. I take my time admiring her. I really admire every single inch of her. From her roped wrists and ankles, to heaving flushed breasts and sweat glistening skin—she is delicious. My fingers close around a toy, a glass dildo. It is cold and the curve is smooth. I know the first touch will be a shock until the glass warms to her body heat.

"Fuck... Yes." Her hands bunch into fists and she moans so fucking loud as I thrust the cold, hard glass into her. She is so wet and it is so smooth, it slides in easily and her body arches and she moans as she accepts it.

I reach up a hand and use my thumb to press against the knot of rope that is tight against her ankle bone. Every thrust and the rope rubs her skin there. She can feel the bind around her wrists that are tied to her ankles as well, and if she reached out with her painted nails, she could just barely rub her fingers against my thumb if she wanted. All this as I fuck her with long strokes. Pounding her, claiming her as mine to toy with. Mine to devour. Mine to fuck.

I don't think she has much but what little control she does have is lost. She cries out, screaming with pure need and pleasure every time I thrust the hard glass toy into her. Her ankles and wrists burn with every writhe of her body. Of course she tries to reach for me. She is desperate for any touch. But she's helpless.

I can see her body beginning to tense, her orgasm is coming. It's there; I can see it written all over her body, and then I hear her voice, no more than a whisper, "Can I come? Please, please can I come?"

I lean forward and touch my thumb to her clitoris while I continue to thrust with the dildo. "Come for me. Come for me like a good girl," I command. And just as her orgasm crashes over her, I pull the dildo from her and press my tongue against her clitoris. I want to taste her. Her climax erupts everywhere and I lose myself in the taste of her and the sweet sweet sound of her pleasure.

I need my own orgasm and I reach to my own clitoris with the fingers of my right hand. I'm soaking wet and my clitoris is more responsive than I have ever known it.

My orgasm comes quick and hard and I moan into it as it shudders through me. I'm lost in the sensation, feeling it ripple through me until I hear her, begging, "Let me taste. Please." I make her stretch her tongue out and beg before I give her my fingers to suck on.

I lean down so I can suck and mark her neck, something primal within me desperately wants to mark her flesh as mine. "My good girl," I say before my teeth bite her flesh.

I move to her mouth. It takes seconds, or minutes, maybe hours, to stop kissing her. Once I finally come back to my senses, I untie her slowly. Adoringly. Massaging her hands and feet lightly with my thumbs as I slip the rope knots undone and free her from her binds.

"Are you ok?" I ask her gently and she nods.

She looks fragile, but content. "So much more

than ok." she murmurs and looks at me with warmth in her gaze.

She moves her hands slowly, testing them out, feeling the blood flow again. I know she must ache and be sore. The marks are there on her body, but they are minimal. Nothing I have done was intended to cause pain or damage to her in any way, merely to add to the feeling of restraint and control.

She looks up at me with those wide green thick lashed Dahlia eyes and I melt. My heart explodes and I scoop her up into my arms. I pull her tight against my chest so she can feel her skin against mine as I carry her into the bathroom.

I hold her as the tub fills, the water hot and steaming, shimmering vapes of coconut heaven filling the room. At first, we don't speak, not with words anyway. Just touches and looks, having spent so long tied, her fingers are now in overtime. They touch me everywhere. Lightly, softly, as though I will vanish from her at any moment.

But I won't. I am not going anywhere.

I overfill the bath but I don't care; I want every inch of her covered and soothed. I lower her in gently. I watch her soft skin sink below the bubbles. She tenses a little. I feel the heat of the water on my arms, and I know it is hot, but not too hot, it will take a minute for her to adjust.

And then her smile spreads and her eyes close as she relaxes in her soapy bliss. I move around a little, opening the cabinet under the sink until I find a new flannel. I add some expensive looking liquid soap and make my way to the bottom of the bath.

I adoringly wash every single inch of her beautiful body. I take tender loving care of her wrists and her ankles to make sure that I don't irritate her skin, I need to soothe it. My hands work their way up and down her legs with the soft flannel, each time she raises them up, steam curls from her freshly pinked skin. I could eat her.

But my touches are not sexual. Even as the flannel glides between her legs and up and over her breasts, the movements are slow and with care. I want her, of course, I want her, but I need her to feel my attention for something more than just sex. I need to caress her with my love for her. This is the part of BDSM that so many don't understand. This time of aftercare only strengthens our bond and our connection, cementing the trust between us so we have a solid foundation to build off each time. I need her trust; I need her to have total faith that I will take care of her even when she is at her most vulnerable.

My mind begins to wander again to what we have. To all that we could maybe be, but my grandmother's words from before ring truer than ever.

The moment we are in is all we ever have. So, I throw myself into that with all the love that I have and hope that it will be enough to show Dahlia all we could be.

11

"Wake up sleepy," I say with a giggle as I nuzzle under the soft, silky, white sheets to a perfectly naked and sleeping Dahlia. She ignores me, or she doesn't wake, either way, I am persistent. Covering her in kisses as my nose nudges at her. She awakens slowly, groggily. Her body probably still aching from the night before, but I know she can still feel those tingles too. And as her eyes flutter open and her morning comes into focus, she smiles.

"What time is it?" she asks, and her voice is dipped in sleep, making my heart flutter.

"It is barely six. The sun hasn't risen yet, but I

wanted to show you something if you want to take a ride with me." I try to keep my tone light, but I am hopeful. I don't have anywhere to call my own. Nowhere in the city is mine, my grandmother's home is home but then it is her home more than anything, adapted for me, but never quite mine. But there is one place I would share with her. A special place.

"Of course, I would love to."

We both get up and dress quietly, there is always a special feeling in the air when you feel like you wake up before the city does. Like you have a secret and you have to keep it to yourself so as not to wake the others and it can then stay just yours a little longer. I linger at the window, watching the lights begin to flicker on around me. Another day almost ready to begin, I wonder what it will bring for them. For us. For me.

Dahlia takes my hand with the slightest rub of her thumb against my palm, and I am transported. Submission is a gift, a beautiful gift that cannot ever be compared, but others are fools to think I hold the power as the dominant one; I am like butter in her hand as she guides me to the elevator. As our bodies rest effortlessly against each other, I worry I am already too far gone with my feelings for her.

The driver is there waiting at the parking elevator, he gets out the moment the doors ping open and I linger as Dahlia enters the open door, murmuring the instructions on where to go.

It is early, but Dahlia is still careful. Her hair is tied back, her sweater loose, and her face half-hidden away by a soft scarf that makes my mind wander to dark and dangerous games we could play right here in the backseat of the car.

She smirks at me as if she can read my mind and says with a dark grin, "I feel like you are kidnapping me, should I be afraid for my life?" she asks with mock panic and I laugh.

"Maybe you would need to worry more if the driver was on my payroll and not yours."

"Hmmm." She leans in, her eyes flashing, "But how do I know you haven't paid him off and this isn't all some big ruse to steal me away in the middle of the night, tie me up and have your wicked way with me ... oh wait..." she says with a tilt of her head. "You already did that. Repeatedly and with my full consent."

I smile. "I had more than your consent. I had your total and utter obedience." I lean in this time, closing in on her lips, my teeth bared, taking a tiny nip at her bottom lip, holding on and then pulling with a light tug. "And I can have it any time again that I choose ... so don't you forget it."

I can see her face turn, the look of submission lingering on her features. I could take her now, I could guide her into that state of obedience, of wanting to give, and I would enjoy every heavenly second. But I don't. Instead, my bite turns into a kiss of softness and I pull back slowly to rest against the seat.

"I want you; you know that, but we have time later. For now, I just want to share something with you." I pause and wonder now if this is a good idea, if I am sharing too much perhaps. But Dahlia's fingers thread with mine and she gives me a light squeeze.

"I can't wait to see something that is special to you."

∿

I don't come here very often, which makes me feel disappointed in myself because I know I should. It is a beautiful spot, way out of the city, past the suburbs when my grandmother lives, and out into the green fields of the countryside. It is the good thing about a small country—it doesn't take much drive time for the landscape to begin to change.

As we reach the off-road dirt parking lot, I am happy that the sunrise still lingers on the horizon, soft pinks, oranges, and reds paint the waking sky.

The car pulls to a slow roll and I can tell the driver is nervous about the lack of people and security.

"Ma'am, I am not sure—" he starts, half turned to talk to Dahlia, but she cuts him off in a second.

"I will be fine. I will be with Alexa and you can see us from outside the vehicle at all times. No need for undue worry. I doubt there is a crazed Dahlia Dante fan out here in the bushes," she says with a playful smile, but I see that it doesn't ease the driver's concern.

"You will be able to see us at all times, but I assure you it is a very quiet spot."

He looks at me and studies my face for a second and then nods, and I wonder if maybe I am the security concern.

We leave the car at different sides then meet in the middle and head down the path.

"I guess that you know about me. The file that Mr. Suit wrote about me was pretty comprehensive, but I think there is a difference between words on paper and a story of a life. So, I thought, we might not have much time for you and me. I know that your life is going to head off soon in another direction and mine probably won't." I don't mean to sound bitter but I fear there is an edge to my voice. "Anyway, I just wanted to share something that I have never shared with anyone, so when the time comes and we have to go our different ways that I gave you something real. A real part of me."

"Alexa..." Her voice trembles a little bit and she is beautiful and vulnerable. "I will come back. I come to London all the time. It will be okay, we can—"

"Shush," I say, softly placing a finger to her lips. "It is okay, I can live in the moment," I murmur as the clearing opens wide and I watch Dahlia's eyes light up as she takes in the lake.

"Oh, it is beautiful," she says in awe.

"Walk with me?" I ask, and she squeezes my hand extra tight.

"It would be my pleasure."

We talk a long, slow walk around the lake. It isn't very big but we amble, taking our time. I start to talk but we have moments. Pauses to take in the flowers, the water, the sunrise. Peppering words with tender kisses and gentle touches.

"I didn't know my parents; I was so young when they died. Not even two years old. So, I don't have memories, I have photographs and stories. When I was a kid, their friends used to tell me about them. I didn't really understand that much then, some stories stay with you, but life goes on and those friends got their own families and maybe they think about my mom when they see hear her favorite song, or my dad when his birthday comes around. Maybe they wonder about me, that sadness, poor Alexa, I wonder what she is doing with herself these days. But it faded away, the visits, the phone calls, the cards. This place is where I feel my mom and dad, where I know them. This is where they got married. My mom was already pregnant with me. My grandmama is traditional like that and she ushered my father into it a little. But they have it on video, not the wedding itself. I don't think they much cared for the church part, but the after-party they had here. At the side of the lake. There are other videos of them together, other moments captured. But the wedding tape is hours and hours of laughter, dancing, singing, smiling, and it is just filled with love. I feel like I was there, that I knew them on that day. So, when I want to be close to them. I come here."

I feel so stupid. I haven't cried about my parents in a long time, but a tear leaks from the corner of my eye and streaks my cheek. Dahlia notices but she doesn't move to stop it.

"I think that we all have a loss, a sadness that we carry around with us. Some people just know life without it and then it hits them. Others, they carry it all their lives and know no different. Your parents sound like lucky people in one way. To have love, you, happiness. I don't know if that makes it better or worse."

"I think better, I try and see the positive in that, they had a happy life. They don't carry the sadness, and I haven't had to carry it alone. I too have been lucky to have my grandparent to help bear the weight with me."

"I didn't have anyone really. I know..." Dahlia pauses, "Mr. Suit can be an asshole, but he is the only one really who has been there. His interest in my wellbeing is selfish, but it is there always. I hadn't had that for a long time and now I don't know what I would do without him."

The sun begins to shine warm and bright, slowly climbing the sky. Our hands are threaded together as we head off the path and into the meadow. The tall grass tickles against her bare legs, Dahlia's dress is light and made of cotton, delicate flowers printed across it; she has taken her big sweater off and the light dances across her skin. As we reach the clearing, I take out a blanket and bring it to my nose, it smells of cherry blossom soap powder. I smile at her with a shy smile and spread it out on the grass, watching her as she lays out on it, more beautiful than ever in the golden morning light. She shakes her lovely red hair loose.

"My marriage, as I am sure you can now understand was just a publicity thing. I am obviously gay and not the only one in that marriage that was. He was nice in the beginning. No, correction, he *acted* nice in the beginning but it didn't last. But I had a contract and I had to fulfill it for my side of the deal to stand. So I did. I put up with it, I played my part. But it was torture. A nightmare. A million miles from where I am now. Here with you."

I feel so shy. The soft blush rises to my cheeks instantly, there is no rope to hide behind here. My fingers carry a tiny tremble as I take a tense deep breath, my eyes finding hers. That moment when they meet, I feel mine well up with tears again. Pure uninhibited emotion.

As her soft sweet voice continues my hips start to sway softly. I circle my ankles, shake off my shoes and feel my pink-painted toes run through the grass.

The thin straps of her dress rest against her collarbone. Her summer tan already faded, her skin is soft and creamy, just the tiniest kiss of the sun still lingering. Her dress blows in the wind and goosebumps line her skin. My confidence grows under her watchful gaze and I bite my lip as I pull the strap from her shoulders.

Her dress doesn't just fall, it clings to her breasts, hugging her body tight so I have to peel it from her skin. The slow reveal of full firm breasts, her nipples are still soft for a brief moment but hardening almost instantly, the breeze caressing them. Following the curves of her body, the dip of her waist, and the flare of her hips, my fingertips continue their undoing.

My hands glide down my clothes and I start to undress myself, peeling away my clothes before meeting her. My palms move to her thighs, her dress finally falls and she is naked. No panties. Just her. Her instinct is to cover, her hands already sliding between her legs to cup her shy but wanting pussy, arms moving across her breasts. But my look stops her.

I lower slowly onto my knees, moving towards her. Making my way up her body, my breasts sway a little with each movement, and I feel my body bared to the elements, nature's gentle kiss on my skin. I wonder if she can see in my eyes how I feel, how she makes me feel.

She holds herself up on her elbows, her thighs together so I can straddle her. My fingers walk up to her chest as I burst into a smile. I rest, hovered slightly above her, my knees bent, sliding wider. Each deep breath makes my breasts rise and fall. My fingers trail through her hair as my thumbs run over her cheekbones. She is so beautiful, so American, I grin to myself and also, so mine.

Cupping her face, I bring Dahlia to me as I move to her. Always in sync, we share a soft, light kiss. Our lips barely moving, the gentle touch of her breath on mine, just offering each other a tender caress and the promise of a thousand more. "You give me butterflies," I whisper softly to the breeze and I lose myself in her.

12

My feet pound the pavement beneath me. I try to keep focused but the thoughts whirl and swirl. I don't want a relationship. I want to win medals. I want to be an athlete. I want an apartment that I don't have to share with assholes. I want, I want, I want. The list is long and the needs are there. I am desperate for a change in my life. But love? Love isn't something I even know how to give.

Except no matter how much my brain rejects the notion and pushes it to one side to discard it, the facts remain. I can feel it inside me. She is all I can think about. I can taste her on my lips. Hear her voice in my head. She plays on repeat even when I am trying not to think about her, and all the time we are apart, I crave her.

I am falling in love with Dahlia Dante.

"I don't get it, Alexa… You have the form, you have the fitness, you have the willpower, but you are distracted, unfocused. You are making mistakes, setting the wrong pace, taking the corners wide, you nearly clipped your heels on that turn there and yet you've made it cleanly for at least ten years. However, your speed is more than I have ever seen, you are getting better and better times. If you can get your focus back and run at this pace… I feel like we are there. But what is wrong? Why can't you focus?"

I stop and bend over, doubled as my lungs cry at the lack of air, my muscles burning, and I feel the spasms. But also, I feel a sense of achievement because Andy is right. I am running faster, setting new personal bests, and I can't explain the change. I just have more energy, more power, more drive. But … less focus.

"I don't know, Andy. I guess it's just life. You know me, I have always put everything into this, but recently, I have been …"

"Living?" he finishes for me as I falter, and I look at his knowing face.

"As your coach and trainer, I am pissed. You have... oh, I don't even want to think about this, but you have, like... days to get this together. On the other hand ... watching you have something other than this in your life makes me really happy."

I reach for him and I pull him into a sweaty hug. He stiffens at first and then he relaxes. We have never hugged before. Even though I feel like I have known him all my life, we have never crossed a line or a boundary. But I felt like this was a moment so I took it. He pulls back after a second looking a little sheepish.

"Hugging doesn't mean you get a discount, you know," he says with an awkward smile.

"I feel like we shouldn't do that again," I laugh and he nods, agreeing.

"No, I don't think so but for what it's worth, I am happy to see you so happy. I just want you to pull it all together so you can be happy ... with a gold medal!"

Don't we all.

∼

"Alexa?" Dahlia's voice echoes through my phone with a sultry sexy heat. I am home—if you can call it that—getting some things together. I fall onto the bed, legs half crossed with wet hair and a sudden teenage grin. "Mmhmm."

"I have to fly out of the city. Just for tonight. They want me to make an appearance at a gala in Milan. I said yes because I will be back tomorrow at lunchtime. You can come here, stay here, wait for me. If you want?"

I feel disappointed but also a flush of happiness that she still wants me to be there and spend time at her place and to be waiting for her when she returna. But it also gives me an idea …

"I can wait for you, but you will be staying at a hotel in Milan tonight?"

"I will."

"I will be over to the hotel later and when you get back after your gala, you should call me."

"Oh?" she purrs with a question in her tone. "You have something you want to talk about?"

"I do, urgent matters that can't be put off any longer."

"Well, I shall make it my number one priority. Also, what is your favorite color?"

"Erm …" I lay back on the bed, my mind blank

of normal thought and instead filled with the erotic. "I guess a deep shade of teal ... one when you can't decide if it is more blue or more green."

"Noted. I will call you later. Oh, and you can look out for me if you like, I will be on television."

She lets it hang there and the phone cuts.

Of course she will be on television.

I can't believe I am having sexual relations with a superstar, who is and will be on TV tonight for a fancy gala thinking about me, but my thoughts are interrupted by my door swinging open.

"Milly! What on earth are you doing in my room without knocking?!" I exclaim.

She at least has the decency to look sheepish.

"Oh, Alexa, I didn't know you were in. I, erm, heard some noises and I thought someone had come in. Maybe they were robbing you or you know, something," she mumbles, half reversing out of the door, except I know full well she had been heading straight for my wardrobe. I have no idea what I have in there that would be of any use to Milly, but what the hell, I'm feeling generous.

"Just take what you came to borrow and not give back, Milly. I don't care, just knock next time."

I watch her stop mid quick exit and look at me with surprise. "For real?"

"Yes, but I can't guarantee I will be in such a good mood next time."

She doesn't hesitate, she's across my room in seconds, diving into my wardrobe to the very back where she has obviously hidden my designer sports coat so she can take it when she pleases. I raise an eyebrow but say nothing, and she doesn't stick around to see if I'll change my mind. She darts out of my room in around two seconds, and a minute later I hear the front door clatter close so I know she has made her quick exit.

To be fair, I had forgotten I even owned that coat, and it may have been expensive but it is ten years old. Oh god, does that make it retro? Am I already vintage? I don't allow my mind to linger on that thought. I instead get up and carry on packing a small bag. I don't need much. I have everything there I need and more, I just need the reality check more than anything. The reminder that this is my home, my reality, and that isn't going to change anytime soon. No matter how much my feelings have begun to blossom.

∼

It's strange walking to the hotel but not going there to work. My few days off have turned into nearly two weeks and yet I spend more time at the hotel right now than I did when I was getting paid. The staff never acknowledge me; it's like they feel I have turned to the dark side. I wonder how it will feel when I return, which I'm due to next week after my big race. Maybe I will transfer. I don't know if I can continue to...

My mind drifts down a dark path, facing the inevitable ending of whatever this is between me and Dahlia and I'm not ready. It makes it hard to breathe to even think about it. So, I switch lanes. Turning my attention to the night ahead. I slip the key card in the slot and press the button for the 85th floor. It takes a minute... But the light flashes green and I begin to rise up the building. As the dial climbs higher, my heart beats faster.

I'd like to say I was productive, but actually, I lazed, daydreamed, took a bath, stared out the window, thought about her. I have clothes here, but I prefer hers. I like smelling her on my skin. I glance at the clock and I know she is due to call and that's how I wait for her. Laid across the bed in her shirt half-buttoned, skimming my bare skin.

The room is dark. Just the city lights from the floor to ceiling glass lighting up the room.

The call comes through and I rest up against the pillows.

"Hey, you," I say softly with a smile in my voice.

"Hey, you too," she replies with her sweeter than honey southern drawl.

"I saw you. On the TV." I didn't just see her, I paused the screen and studied her like an obsessively hooked voyeur. There were a million things to be drawn to. Some people on the red carpet shimmered, but she shone like the only star in an ink black night.

A single beam lit up the red carpet. Mist rose, seeping around the shadowed photographers in black, their faces obscured, who they were completely unimportant, there to capture not to be noticed. Her eyes were closed with sweeping dark lines of makeup brushed over her eyelids. I watched her step in high heels to the center of the carpet, her gown flowing behind her in a sea of green-blue. Her lips were deep cherry red and I could almost feel them on my skin as her eyes opened and she smiled for the camera.

"You looked sensational. You stole the show in every way possible. I saw you on all the best dressed lists already. How did you do it so quickly? Get the dress that color?"

I could hear her shrug down the line. "I ask and people do. I wanted you to know I was thinking about you."

"I like to know you are thinking about me. What are you wearing right now?"

"I just have panties and a shirt. And you?"

"I will show you."

I flick the call to video and I watch the dots wait to connect. I wonder if she will accept but the chime comes and she appears on my screen and I see myself in the small tile on the bottom left corner.

"I am wearing a shirt, but it is yours."

She laughs, "Same." And she directs the camera downwards to show me my own t-shirt, not one she bought me either, a cheap old thing I wore one of the first nights and never thought about again.

"Take it off."

I watch her hesitate. Filming isn't allowed and I wonder if she worries about the rules, but I am not recording. This isn't to keep, it is for now, to enjoy. Then she makes a move to follow my direction but I spot the dresser in the corner of the frame.

"Wait. Go sit there, at the dresser, rest the phone in front of the mirror. I want to see and watch everything. Can you do that for me? Can you be a good girl?"

She gives me a shy smile, a flush rising to her cheeks before she nods, standing. Making her way over.

She sits on the white leather stool at the dressing table. The dark room is lit with the soft yellows of the bulbs that line the frame of the mirror. She leans forwards and I let my gaze sweep over her features. I scan every detail from her lightly curled lashes to full rosy lips.

She gives her head a little shake and bouncy red curls fall forwards to frame her face. Her teeth lightly run over her bottom lip, the softest of bites with just a hint of pressure and she shivers. The light silky fabric of my black shirt slips from her left shoulder. Exposing creamy soft skin, the V spreads downwards, splitting at her chest so the valley of her breasts is on show, the hint of a curve at her full breasts but nothing more.

I feel the pulse between my thighs. Fuck. She is delicious. Heavenly. My mouth salivates just looking at her. "More," I say softly.

She stretches her legs forwards and twirls her

ankles. The shirt rides higher and higher up her thighs, skimming the top, almost high enough for a peek of her sex but not quite. She adjusts on the chair, letting the shirt cover the curve of her ass, a buffer between naked skin and cool leather.

Her eyes close, her breath held as her lips tremble. I am waiting for her touch to watch her fingers trace down her skin. To show me herself and to give me what I ask.

I watch silently as her fingers run down the exposed skin between her breasts until she reaches the last button. Her eyes flash open as the shirt falls open. Her rosy nipples are bared and I watch them harden.

"You are so beautiful. Touch yourself as if it were me. Show me how you want me to take you right now."

She shrugs her shoulder and I watch my shirt fall. It skims her back, falling down the curve of her spine as she pulls her arms free. Naked, all for me.

Her fingers begin to explore. First the nape of her neck, then along her collarbone, the backs of her fingers trace the light outer curve of her breasts before her thumb flicks against her nipple and she moans.

It is intoxicating. A dizzying high. Every time she moves, I too begin to touch myself. Not mirroring, just going to the places my body craves, where I need the touch. Exploring whilst my eyes are focused solely on her.

The ultimate act of voyeurism. I feel the buttons of her shirt against my stomach. Cool cotton against my hot skin. The flush spreads from my chest to my thighs as I watch her palm dip between her legs—cupping, caressing, a possessive grip—before her fingers begin to move.

She watches me now, as I watch her. Our moans fill each other's room. I have never done anything like this before but it is so incredibly sexy. I only want more and more and more.

My body gets there faster than my mind, eyes fixed on her perfect feminine form I give in to the pleasure and I climax for her, just as her own waves of orgasm begin. It is messy, neither of us in sync, the cameras drop.

Dahlia. What are you doing to me?

13

Dahlia returned and we dove into a day of sex and food and movies and just being with each other. It was bliss, I loved her suite, not just the luxury and everything you could want at the end of the phone, but it was the view that captured me the most. I loved it, I spent hours curled up in a chair watching the city pass by. It was better when Dahlia was curled up on me, running lines, reading contracts, practicing accents, but even without her... it was special and I cherished it.

It was the night before my race qualifications. I knew that Dahlia couldn't come and watch me run; it was too public and it would cause too much of a stir, but she had arranged for a car to take me there and promised something special for after, no matter what happened.

I was going through my mental checks and mapping through the course. I had run it a few times, a road course. It had its pros and cons. I prefer street running in terms of terrain and running surface, but I miss the atmosphere of a stadium. This was only the heats, though. I would run the 10k once, in a group I had been preselected for based on my average time last year.

It was an advantage I could exploit because I was racing much faster right now than my average last year, meaning I could sit comfortably in the front pack before using the final thousand with a burst to take a good qualification time.

The key would be to finish with the right time. I had to make sure I qualified without giving myself too much noise. I didn't want to be a target, spotted and stalked in the final.

So, for me, tomorrow would be a purely tactical race, which meant focus. Something that I had been lacking a lot lately. "Alexa, your phone is ringing."

I reach for it on the table but I already know who it is.

"Hey, Grandmama."

"Hello, you. How are you feeling?" I never tell her, but I know when she is nervous. She still has a landline and when she is fretting, she will start to wrap the cord around her palm, fidgeting and it gives the line a distinct rustle.

"I feel good. Andy is pretty happy; I just need focus but the speed and pace are there. I feel good."

"Okay sweetheart. Well, I won't be there tomorrow, but you know I will make it for the final. Call me after. I will be thinking of you, sending you some of my energy, what little of it I have left," she adds with a laugh and I smile.

"Thanks, Grandmama. I will call you straight after and let you know in way too much detail how it went."

"Oh, you know I love all the details. Get lots of sleep tonight. I love you."

"I love you too, sweet dreams."

I hear the line click and I feel Dahlia's gaze on me. "She loves you a lot."

I nod. "She does, I am very lucky. I don't take that for granted."

"You shouldn't, and she shouldn't either,

although I can tell in her tone how much she adores you. She sounds like a very sweet woman."

"She is. The absolute sweetest. Even sweeter than your tea."

Dahlia drops her notepad to look up at me over her cute reading glasses. "Nothing... is sweeter... than Texan iced tea." And from her tone, I'm not going to doubt it.

～

Dahlia would make a perfect wife. To the right person, not her asshole ex. I wake the next morning to a buffet. I struggle to eat on race mornings, but I manage to force some down me because I know I'll need it. She has also laid out a beautiful new running outfit, tracksuit and shoes, I wear the outfit but I don't have the heart to tell her that new shoes would be a terrible idea.

There is a whole kit prepared, which I can only assume someone had been sent to the Nike store and bought everything and anything on the shelf that looked like it might be useful and packed it all into a very fancy sports bag and then a holdall because they didn't all fit in the bag.

"I didn't know what you might need, so I got

you a couple of things," she says shyly with a blush that makes my heart melt.

"It is all perfect. I am sorry you can't be there, but it is incredibly boring for the first 9.5k anyway. All of it will be on a screen."

"I will be watching. I pulled some strings and I will have access here to the live stream. I thought maybe next time I can set that up for your grandmother too, if you want?"

"Oh, Dahlia! She would love that!"

"Well, maybe I can get it done today... leave it with me and I will see what we can have arranged."

"You are an angel. Thank you." She drapes herself slowly over my lap in her favorite position, curled around me with her hands locking around my neck so her nose can nuzzle in. She smells like honey and cinnamon. Her hair is soft against my skin as I take a long, deep inhale.

She will be watching. I suddenly feel like I have a whole new reason to focus.

∼

I don't get nervous before a race, but I do shake. It is the adrenaline, the rush of endorphins. My mind knows what it needs to do and it makes my blood surge, my pulse race, my heart beats faster so I can push myself as hard as I physically can.

My group has Leticia Jones in it, and she is a firecracker of a starter. She will set a high pace, and I just have to keep on her heels and watch the others drift away. Not challenging, just letting her set the speed. It makes it easier for me in the long run, but it is always difficult to sit back when you have a lot more gas in the tank. Which is exactly what I am doing now. We are 7k in. Resting on her heels, the urge to push her, to come round her on the outside and drive this front pack forwards... but I focus, remembering the tactics. Knowing I need to only just win, not set records.

There is a scuffle. It is every runner's nightmare this kind of race. A clipped heel, a shoulder, then suddenly you feel the sting of gravel as you hit the floor. Precious seconds are lost and then you risk injury, your vitals plummet, you lose the pace. All your training has gone in a second.

I keep myself compact, my arms in tight, eyes scanning my surroundings, but I pass the scuffle unscathed. Our leading pack of nine is now down to six. Better or worse is yet to be seen, but I think it could be in my favor. Less to compete within the final stretch.

Leticia is a great starter and the big names will want her to make it to the final because she pushes them to set records. For the first 8K, she is unstoppable, but then she begins to tire. She can keep it up to some extent, she finishes well, often pushing for a medal; I am sure her cabinet is filled with bronzes but she doesn't have the speed at the finish to get the gold.

I have raced with Leticia many times and keeping her pace for the first 8K is tough. It has always been fifty-fifty as to whether I will keep up with her. But today, my attitude is different. I have no doubt, had no doubt coming here, and it shows in my running. I am not *trying* to keep up, I just am.

We break the 8k mark and I feel the slackened pace. I ride it for another 1000m just making sure that we are keeping good time so we are challenging the other heats. And then I make my break for it.

I don't want to storm ahead, but I feel my legs dip into the reserves, and there is a lot left in the tank. My stride is strong, powerful. My muscles are tight but not cripplingly so. I have full control of my breathing. My body is functioning at the highest possible level and it isn't breaking, it is soaring.

The meters count down. I don't know how far I have cleared, but with a quick glance back I can breathe a sigh of relief. Leticia is not far behind; she is keeping up and that is exactly where I want to be, in front but not by a long stretch. I trust in my sprint finish that I can beat Leticia.

I clear the last straight in what feels like slow motion in my head. It has been a long time since I crossed a finish line first and I revel in it. Enjoying every second of how it feels to win my heat. Andy is there, I can see him beaming from the sidelines. I don't have anyone else, but I know they are only a phone call away.

Whilst I catch my breath, dousing myself in water, I reach for my personal bag and take out my phone, which bursts into a life that very second.

"Hey, Grandmama," I pant.

"Oh, Alexa! I saw you! I can see you now on the TV! A lovely gentleman came round and set the whole thing up for me, said it was a special gift from you! Thank you so much, I can't believe it. I can see you on my screen right now talking to me!"

I hear a scuffle as she leans away from the landline to look at me talking to her on the TV and I laugh.

"I'm happy you were able to see! And now you are going to see me in the final in four days! Can you believe it!?"

"Yes," she replies seriously. "I had no doubt, you should know that. Now go and call your special friend and tell her the good news." I blush and laugh.

"Thanks, Grandmama. I love you."

"I love you too sweetheart. You have made me so proud."

I feel like my smile splits my face as I hang up and dial Dahlia. She answers in seconds, screaming, cheering—a ball of heated excitement. It feels so nice to have someone to share in my joy. She is talking at a hundred miles an hour, and all it does makes me want to get back to her as soon as possible and cover her in a million kisses.

And I can hear it in her voice that she wants exactly the same thing.

14

The lights are off as day turns into the night whilst we lie naked in the bed, the room darkens as the sun goes to sleep, but the soft moonlight and city stars illuminate our space. This perfect place we've found ourselves in. And in an instant, our limbs tangle, and her body is pulled against mine ...my heat is given to her, brushing her hair from her face as I stare into her clear green eyes.

I softly bite my lip, my heart is racing, pounding in my chest. She takes me to the most wondrous of places. As her thumb runs over my lip, I don't lick or suck, just feel the softness, my gaze rising to hers and in a moment, things just melt away. Moving into her arms is seamless. Gaps close effortlessly until my sex brushes her thigh and I feel the hot wetness of hers against my own thigh. I can't explain the closeness, the intimacy. It's overwhelming and yet at the same time, could never be too much.

I love you.

I nearly say 'I love you', every part of me aches to voice the words in my head, but I choose to let the words linger unspoken.

I do love her. I know now that I have loved her for a while, perhaps even since the start. This is different, so very different and so much more than anything I have felt before.

My thumb stretches her lip down and I look at her neat white teeth and her gums, memorizing every part of her. I feel the wave of heat from her sex as she settles up against me, the slow tingle of my sex as I meet her soft touch. Fuck, she makes it so easy. She turns me on so quickly and makes me want to consume her. I dip my lips, still pulling hers down, and kiss her top lip and her exposed, perfectly white teeth. A soft, tender kiss only letting go of her bottom lip once we are joined so it completes the seal.

She smiles coyly, trying to play it cool. But she

is beaming. The kind that makes her eyes sparkle, her cheeks blush. I'm happy, so happy. Kissing her back is like poetry. Our lips move together and against, tiny tastes are taken, touches given, my palms rise to her face and I trace her eyebrows, skim her eyelashes, her fine cheekbones, following her jaw as my nails run through her silky red hair. I want to touch every inch, every millimeter of her. *Mine*, I think to myself. All the time our bodies move too. Like magnets, closing gaps, skin brushing, teasing, toying.

Every movement is perfect harmony as we respond to the touch of the other all in the midst of perfect kisses that grow and explore and comfort. Our hands wrapped around the other's body, my fingertips memorizing every bump on her back, the curves of her waist and hips. I lift her leg and direct her to wrap it around me. Those long legs drive me crazy. Fuck ...I could kiss her forever.

Her leg slides slowly up my outer thigh, her heel trailing up the back of my legs. Her pussy, pressed against my thigh, parts, and I feel her blossom. Her lips spread and her folds give me that first kiss of a wet touch. Just a hint . But I know the moment I touch her with my fingers, she will be dripping; that's how she is every single time. My need to have her is overwhelming and as her leg settles, I pull her against me harder and she gives my lip a light nip of teeth.

I love the light nips. I love the sharp bites. I love it all. All of what she gives me. My hands graze against her back until I feel the thick-down comforter that rests on her hip. Grabbing it and pulling it high over her head and giving us our little private tent, I roll flat onto my back and bring her on top of me. From one side, the light struggles to shine through the duvet from outside the massive window. Thousands of twinkling lights and lives being lived just beyond the glass, but here, under these crisp white sheets, it's me and her. And as she settles on top of me and my arms wrap around her again, we fit perfectly together.

"Heaven," she murmurs.

Our tent. Our place. Words fail me for a minute. Dahlia is on top and straddling me—except it's more being part of me. Her fingers tangle in my hair as she kisses me again and again. Heat rises under the covers, our bodies responding to each other as that urgency starts to grow.

My fingertips never stop moving against her skin. My deep carnal need for the flesh is something that I always have. But Dahlia... Fuck. It is all the time. Her flesh is my food—and my animal is always hungry. I pull and tug at her body, feeling her stretch in the most intimate of places.

Her neediness erupts—this slow burn has pushed her to no control. Her hands slide down, nails raking my sides, and she catches my hands. She takes them and slides our hands upwards, above my head, fingers escaping the covers. And she rises up just a little, her nose brushing mine as she rocks against my body, sliding back and forth, her breasts swaying, catching against my chest as she holds my hands tight. I know she feels the quickening of my breath.

Her breasts sway dangerously close to my face and my chin tickles her delicate and perfect pink nipples—nipples that beg to be adored, to be licked, teased, nibbled.

I gladly let her take my arms as she pleases, but knowing that our neediness is taking over I push the comforter off and tilt my head to the right, barely able to let her breasts go for the moment, and look down the bed, past us, and see our reflection in the giant mirror. Her round ass is settled upon me, the darkness is between us but I can see that beautiful glisten on my thighs, she isn't even touching me, but I just know I'm close to orgasm. I look up at and meet her gaze and we both know the moment is coming. I motion with my eyes and a little flick of my chin for her to look back and watch; watch in the mirror that magical moment when we come together.

She knows what she wants, what she needs; her body tells her and she follows it without question. She releases my hands and her body settles back as she gives my lips one last deep kiss. And then she rises up and grinds against my pelvis and the city lights paint her skin. Flashes of amber, whites, yellows, and reds across her beautiful body. Her breasts sit heavily with her flushed, hard nipples.

It doesn't matter how many times we have done this—each time is like the first when I'm with her.

But at the same time, we know each other's body so well now.

My fingers rake up her thighs, traveling up to her breasts and taking them in a full grip and seeing just how full they can be as I push them together. I look up at her as she edges us closer and closer.

"God. You are so. Fucking. Sexy."

You drive me completely insane.

She is exquisite.

I'm not the only one so deeply affected. Dahlia undulates her body against mine. "I needs you," she breathes, barely more than a whisper. "You make me crazy," she moans with the softest mews.

She raises both hands up catching her hair, holding it up, her breasts rise higher, pulled firmer, stretching her body out. And I am utterly intoxicated.

I let my hands fall so I can soak her in completely. My palms are resting on her thighs just above the knees and I watch her facial expression as she throws her head back and grinds her hips on mine. My hands move down to her ass and grip her tightly as we rock together.

Her eyes find mine.

I love it. I am starting to shake, vibrating as I climb higher and higher.

She leans her body down onto me, still gripping me tightly with her legs. Her hands pull me tightly against her. I want to say it, but I don't. She can tell by my breathing, those deep breaths that vibrate up against her neck as I kiss my way upward, I'm close—so close. My hands swipe through her hair and clench in ecstasy.

Her lips meet mine.

Our climax begins together and never seems to fade. Time has no meaning. Tears stream down her cheeks. Her senses are overwhelmed to the point of incomprehensible euphoria. I am floored. Lost in Dahlia Dante so deep I am drowning.

I love you. I love you. I love you.

"I love you," I murmur against her lips.

I don't think I meant to say it, but the words fell out of my mouth like the most natural thing in the world.

I don't have any more words. Slowly, like we're floating on air, which we are, I roll us onto our sides—still facing, still joined— lost in gentle kisses. A million people could be watching us or no one. It doesn't matter.

"My Running Queen," she whispers with a sigh against me, and I beam with pride and exhaustion.

"I love you too."

I should win more often.

15

"I am not going to lie; you ran a perfect race."

"Well, thank you, Andy, for saying so," I laugh as sweat pours off my skin.

"But... Friday is different. All the rules are different now, okay?" he says with an edge in his voice as I drop to the floor and continue my gym session, moving to pushups.

"You ran the perfect heat race but now you need to win the final. You have to play the first 8k very similar. Sit on the heels of the leader. Leticia is probably going to lead again and expect her to go out faster and stronger. You surprised her in the heat; she didn't think you had that finish in you after the pace she had set so she is going to set it higher. Then you also have the rest of the group. That front pack of eight... you can expect that to be 12 this time, and they are all there to win. Keep your body in tight, keep the pace, push through that pain, and find your stride. And then the final 2k... you have to go for it, Alexa. *Do not wait.* Get out in front and win that race early. If you wait, someone will go past you at the end. There are girls in that field with faster finishes than you. Make them come for you when you go hard in the last 2K; you have so much energy, use it, pour it out. That gold is yours if you want it, so you take it, okay?"

I nod through gritted teeth. I am going to take it or do all I can to get myself there. Grandmama will be there and I know Dahlia is pulling out all the stops to make sure she can be there at the finish line too. I'm not holding my breath; it is not a big event by celebrity standards, but there will be cameras, TV coverage, and a sky sports highlight throughout the day. It is a risk for Dahlia, and Mr. Suit is not too fond of the idea. But I have a feeling Dahlia will get her own way.

For a woman who has submissive traits in the bedroom, she certainly knows how to get things done her way outside of it—and all with a smile and southern class. I am in awe of her constantly. That is not something I try to hide in the slightest and I worry my feelings are too clear. I wonder if it is only a matter of time before we both sit down and had a conversation about what we are doing and what our options are.

I punished myself through a grueling training and then spent hours studying my rivals. Going over and over my tactics. I was going to do this. I could feel it in my bones that I was ready and I knew the tingles of love that I felt were only adding to my confidence in my ability to win.

~

The early morning sun sneaks through the curtains and stretches out on the pillow next to Dahlia. Slowly creeping closer until it finally caresses the softness of her cheek, prompting her sea-green eyes to flutter open. She blinks herself awake and smiles at the sight of the gift next to her. A clutch of wildflowers smiles back at her tucked carefully under the ribbon wrapped around the simple, white box.

She sits up, her red hair, messy from sleep, brushes her shoulders as she pulls the gift into her lap, fingering the velvet petals of the flowers before bringing them to her face, inhaling their sweet scent. She sets them aside and tugs the emerald ribbon, releasing the bow. Taking a deep breath, she lifts the lid from the box. Her smile widens as she reads my note. I watch her from the bathroom door but I don't make a sound, just drinking in her delight and watching the flush spread as she whispers my words.

"Wear this for me today, my love. It's not nearly as beautiful as you, but it's the best I could do. I can't wait to see you tonight!"

I watch her as she rises to get ready. She has a big meeting today, and she chooses her outfit carefully. The dress caresses her curves like a lover, but the hemline is long enough to be professional. The neckline dips enough to invite the eye, a teasing peek at the bounty beneath the viridian fabric.

She realizes I've been watching and almost shyly thanks me for the gift. There's no time to talk, but we know we'll be together soon. She walks with confidence as she leaves the penthouse, adding a sultry sway to her hips. Her hand raises to finger the charm on her choker. My choker for her.

I have a plan for her today. She has promised me a special night before my race, but I feel like she deserves some attention from me. I am resting my body; my day will be spent in front of the widescreen cinema display, so I have plenty of time to give her attention.

I give her space, time to settle into her day and her meeting. Knowing my charm lingers on her skin. That she will feel the brush of my choker against her throat every time she moves.

I call her around lunchtime. The phone rings and she answers; I can hear her smiling brightly at my voice on the end of the line. I waste no time on small talk, instead adopting the tone that makes Dahlia shiver. "Lock the door, baby, and take those panties off. Put them in your bag. You won't need them again today."

I hear Dahlia gasp, but without question, she sets the phone down. I imagine her standing to lock the door. She'd lean on it for support while pulling her dress up her pale thighs, hooking her thumbs under the lace, and peeling down and stepping out of the panties. I am positive she did what I ordered and they are now stowed in her purse. In just a minute, she has brought the receiver back to her ear, and I know she has followed directions well. "Good girl," I murmur, and I swear I can almost feel her pulse racing through the phone.

Dahlia takes a deep shuddering breath. "Spread your legs for me... trail your fingers along your inner thigh. Start at your knee and slowly drag your nails higher"

She whimpers, I know she yearns for my touch, I know she will follow my instructions. "Touch yourself. With one finger. Tease yourself."

Her breath quickens and I can hear the shift of fabric. "Rub your clitoris," I encourage through the phone. "Good girl, tease yourself. I hope you are wet for me." Deep, quickening moans are her only reply.

"One finger, baby. Just one. Push it inside yourself." I imagine Dahlia arched against her hand, wet and aching for me. "Two now ... get there, baby." Her pussy will tighten around her fingers as she curls them forward. Her thighs will tremble. I'm sure her breathing is telling me she's getting closer.

"Now... stop, my love. Wait. No orgasm until I see you." She gasps and whimpers, but I know she obeys. "Yes, Alexa," she answers, and I can hear the need in her voice.

"But take a taste, taste your sweetness for me."

I can hear her finger swirl around her tongue, the smack of her lips as she sucks, and I feel tingles between my own legs.

Fuck, she is so sexy.

~

I wait for her to return to the bedroom. I've enjoyed watching a movie while she was out and now I want to watch her undress; I want to be a voyeur to her sexiness and she does not disappoint. She reaches behind her, pulls the silver zipper down revealing the smoothness of her skin. First one arm, then the other slips from the sleeves. Her hands slide over her breasts, cupping them, teasing her nipples, thumbs brushing against the sensitive buds until they strain against the midnight lace. She reaches back again, releasing the clasp of the bra. Shrugging thin straps from freckled shoulders, the thin fabric falls to the floor.

My eyes are wide as she urges the dress over the curve of her hips, down until it joins the bra on the floor. She bends to gather the garments, laying them neatly across the back of a chair. Shapely calves lead to creamy thighs, hips that beg to be gripped, and rosy pink nipples that need to be kissed. She admires herself briefly in the mirror before removing her fingers dancing along her collar.

"I prepared the bathroom for us," I say softly, and she turns with a raised eyebrow.

"It was my turn to treat you."

I stand slowly, pushing the door open, letting it swing wide. "You treat me all the time," I murmur.

Dozens of candles light the warm room, filling the air with the gentle scent of lavender and vanilla. Fragrant steam rises from the clawfoot tub in the center of the room as bubbles float lazily on the surface of the hot water. Music plays from the speaker in the corner adding to the calm of the evening.

I feel her follow me; I know she feels the tingles as do I. I gesture with my head to the floor and she kneels there quietly, patiently awaiting a vision of beauty and submission. Her delicate hands rest on the smoothness of her thighs, palms up, offering herself to me. A satisfied smile curves my lips, my heart swells with pride. My woman. My sweet Dahlia.

I step forward and reach a hand down to caress her face. The look of trust in Dahlia's eyes makes my pulse skip. I offer her my hand and pull her up into my arms, fitting her curves easily to mine. I tangle my fingers in her hair and bring her closer, inhaling that soft sweet scent before brushing my lips gently over hers. Savoring the moment, I slip my tongue between her lips seeking the sweetness of her mouth. Quiet moans pass between us as the world falls away.

Unable to resist, my hands roam her body, caressing each dip and curve of form as our tongues dance. I nudge her legs apart and press my thigh between them, chuckling softly at the warmth I find there. Nipping at her lips before breaking our kiss to meet those wide green eyes. "It's been a long day… let me take care of you."

I guide her to the tub and help Dahlia lower slowly into its soothing heat. Her sigh as the water envelops her is my first reward and I let it linger. Smiling, I move behind her to gather her long red hair and secure each silken strand into a messy bun atop her head. My lips press against her pulse and my breath tickles her ear as I whisper, "Mine."

I can feel the shiver that runs through her at the word. My teeth graze her neck, my voice firmer. "Mine." Her wide eyes seek mine as her lips form the breathless reply, "Yours."

"Mmmm, good girl." I begin massaging the tiredness of the week from her weary muscles. My hands are small but strong, my fingers skillful as they find each knot and free her from its bonds. The relaxing scents and sounds surround us and my hands venture ever further. My soft palms cup her full breasts, thumbs tease hardening nipples, hinting at pleasures yet to come.

I stand and walk around the tub, a robe of white silk clings to my body as I move. I can feel her eyes on me even before I turn to face her, my beautiful girl, how she makes my heart race. I watch her reactions carefully as I untie the belt at my waist, as the fabric parts revealing lightly tanned skin dusted with freckles, as I shrug it from my shoulders and let it fall forgotten to the floor.

I pause for a moment to admire her, the elegant lines of her body, the curve of her lips, the depth of her eyes, the way stray wisps of hair curl around her face in the steamy air. Returning to her side, I bend and brush my lips over hers before kneeling next to the tub. My hand slips under the bubbles, fingers find the smoothness of her shin and travel higher.

Higher and higher, along her inner thigh, feeling the soft shivers under my fingertips until finally, they press gently against her sex, her heat challenging that of the bath. I watch her face intently as my thumb circles against her clit, as I slip a finger inside her. And then another. Slow and steady, massaging her most intimate places, the ones I know will make her moan.

My eyes never leave Dahlia's as my fingers move inside, curling gently, coaxing her toward blissful release. Her slickness arouses my own and my attentions become more urgent. She tightens around me, encouraging my touch, and I smile, pulling my fingers from inside her to stroke her gently, prolonging her pleasure. Her eyes plead with me and I happily give in to her desire.

My fingers slide easily back into her needy sex, my palm pressed firmly against her clit. It pulses beneath my hand as fingers pull her toward the edge of release, calling her orgasm from her core. Smiling softly when I feel her start to tremble and quake. "That's right, Dahlia. Come for me. Let it go, baby."

Her body tenses for a moment, suspended on the precipice before tumbling into gasping, blinding oblivion. I hold her tight as each wave washes through her, flooding over my hand. "Good girl, baby. Sweet perfect girl." Again, I slowly withdraw my fingers, gently stroking her sex before leaning forward to kiss her nose. Standing, I slip into the tub behind her and wrap my arms around her, sighing happily as we relax together.

Her hands lightly wander but I am not looking for my own release, I don't seek the highs of my climax. It is high enough just to hold her tight in my arms and feel her skin on mine.

"It doesn't matter what happens tomorrow," she whispers with a dreamy sigh. "I love you with or without the gold."

And suddenly, it feels like I have already won all I have ever wanted.

16

"Grandmama, this is my friend Dahlia," I introduce her with caution, but I needn't bother. Dahlia steps in and swoops her up in a long deep hug that envelopes my grandmother's frail old bones in a wrap of warmth, and I know she is instantly bathed in the electric heat of what it feels like to be in Dahlia's presence.

"Thank you for the television wizardry you did for me. It was very kind of you. The nice gentleman even helped me record it. Watched her win that race at least five times this week." My Grandmama smiles and I blush.

"Just the heats," I correct her, "I still need to win the race today."

We are at the family and friends' enclosure; I had made my own way to the track with Andy for last-minute prep and strategy talk. Grandmama had taken a private car sent by Dahlia, but Dahlia had made her own way incognito so as to try and not draw attention to the fact she was here.

I could see her a mile away—no dark clothes, sunnies, or dark Nike cap could hide her distinctive body and smile, but it seemed to be working. People were not exactly expecting a Hollywood movie star at the women's European athletics 10k final.

The next hour passes for me in a blur. I have to switch off from my thoughts of Dahlia. I can't process that she and my Grandmama are sitting together, talking, chatting, watching from the sidelines. I have to focus. This is my dream. This is what I have worked for for so many years.

It is different to run in a stadium. For me, it is the best way to compete in a final. The adrenaline the crowd gives you is unparalleled. When you are street running, you see the pavements lined with supporters but your loved ones only get a glimpse. For only a few seconds, you can hear them; you listen for their tone, their voice through the cheers and it gives you a huge push.

In the stadium, you can't single them out, but you know they are there the whole time. You can feel their eyes on you, following every step that you take. For some people, they zone that out, it brings nerves and pressure and deflects from the focus needed to win.

But today I felt empowered, bolstered by the fact that the only two people in the world that I loved were here, together, side by side, watching me.

I complete my testing, go through the pre-race checks and make my way to the start line. Running a 10k is 25 laps around the stadium. It doesn't seem so many... but it is, I will feel every grueling second.

We line up with no real order. It is always the way in the longer distance races. Take a spot on the line then fall into the inner curve. The gun goes and I feel the bang vibrate through my bones, but I am moving instantly without a thought.

I find the rhythm. The place in my mind to retreat to. It is all I can do now—let my race instinct kick in whilst I follow the race strategy. I am confident in my stride and keep my body tight as I make my way to the front pack. This first lap is crucial in sitting in the right position and I find it perfectly.

My coach was right. The group is bigger this time. Eleven of us and I am sitting on the edge around sixth. It has its advantages. I am less likely to be clipped, I am not trapped in the inside. But for every lap, I run further than the others and that will catch up with me quickly. So, I have to keep on the heels of Leticia and force her to keep a faster pace so that the punishing early speed will make a few drop off.

The pace is intense. I feel the burn from the third lap. Sweat runs down my body and glistens on my skin as I feel my Lycra slicken with perspiration. But I keep up, I keep the push on Leticia, and she responds. She wants that gold too and she tries to outpace me, make me falter early so she can breeze across the line.

But, I want it more. This time around I want it more than I ever have. I don't want to be the 'nearly' athlete anymore.

The pace is blistering and the pack segments. Eleven becomes eight, and then by the fifteenth lap we are down to six. It is unheard of for this distance. We are running a race of unknowns.

Leticia begins to falter and I think she knows she can't hold on. She slows, but it is too early for me to take the lead according to my plan. Too early for Leticia to fade according to everyone else's race plan too I imagine. There is a stumble, a moment of uncertainty. Heels are clipped, ripples of shock spread through the crowds, but I keep to my spot on the outer edge. There is a fall. I don't know who. I can't process. I just have to keep running. Keep going.

Jansen takes the lead. She is Dutch. A gold medal favorite, but I can tell it is a reluctant action from her to take the lead so early. She, too, is running the same race as me and she now has two options. Set a hard fast pace and shake the four of us that remain in the group with her, or conserve her energy and hope she has enough to outsprint us in the final two.

She does exactly what I would do in her position. Which I know my coach would scream at me for after. She goes for it.

She knuckles in, head down, pulling on those reserves to power ahead. The times we are running now must be well above European records. Even maybe World.

Lap 20 comes and goes and my body is utterly

exhausted. The five of us become four. La Zorra for Spain drifts back and there is me, Jansen, Lavigne for France, and Ricci of Italy. Four nations battling it out now for three medals. Jansen has set an unforgiving pace; she has pushed us to the limits and now we all can only slow.

I try and settle into the new rhythm and let my body find that reserve that I should still have. I know the tactic, break away ahead with 5 and a half laps to go. But that is only 800m away and I don't know how much I have left in me. Will I have any speed left in me by that point? Will it be enough to outpace the others? I start to whizz through the possible scenarios in my head and in all of them I feel the gold and silver slipping away. I make a choice to save my push for when there are 2 laps left to go.

As I approach two laps to go, I'm flagging, but I know I must do it. This is my time. I won't get another. I know it. My coach knows it. Even Grandmama knows it in her heart; it is why she is here. And I have to do it.

Not for Dahlia, though I feel her eyes on me with every step I take.

This is for me and for my Grandmama.

I have to do it for the woman who has always

believed in me, who invest her entire life in giving me all she could...

The moment my toe hits the white line with two laps to go. I push.

I have two laps left. 800metres.

I storm ahead of Jansen. I don't know who breaks away with me. I feel the air behind me, though, the relentless pad of shoes on track and I know I am not alone. I want to look back, to see how many have come with me. How close they are. To see the pain in their eyes to know if they can keep up with me, if they want it as much as I do.

The meters count down and I run. I run like I have never run before, and I reach the white line again and the bell chimes. The crowd is on its feet; they have waited for this, the final lap. And I use that energy to push and push.

I feel the brush beside me. Ricci is there, but I have the advantage until the home straight; she has to take the wider corner or power ahead to overtake me, and I can see she is faltering. We are both running on nothing except I am on the inside with the advantage and I take it.

I stride longer, I gain those all-important inches whilst I can. I don't want to bank on her not having the energy for a finish on the straight. I power around the inside. I don't even feel the burn or the ache now. I am delirious, pushing myself to the absolute maximum.

The home stretch. The final straight.

She is there on the outside but that doesn't matter now. We both have 100 meters to go.

We both have the chance. It is ours. Gold or Silver.

I am sure at that moment I hear the two women who love me shouting me home. Maybe it is an illusion. My brain telling me what I need to hear. But I can feel the screams from their lips. My name on their tongues. Love for me in their eyes. I run. I run so hard I feel like my legs will fall off. Like my lungs will give in. As though my heart will stop.

I don't even know. I can't process. I speed past the line and it takes me a second to stop. For my brain to comprehend that it is over, that I have finished my race.

I look up at the board and I wait. It takes an age. I can't breathe even though my body has stopped, my limbs like jelly, and then it flashes on the billboard and the crowd erupts.

Gold: Sharpe Alexa
GBR

*NEW WORLD RECORD 29:00.03**

I feel my legs give from under me, but before I reach the floor, arms scoop me up. A haze of red hair, pale skin, and adoring kisses. She covers me, holding my exhausted frame as she showers me in love.

"Alexa! You did it!" she screams. "You won! You are the fastest in the world! Oh, my goodness, I can't believe it. You were incredible!" She gushes and I smile at her infectious euphoria. Turning, I see Andy and Grandmama making their way over. Slower, but I see they have just as much happiness and pride.

"Oh, Alexa," Grandmama says and bursts into tears. Dahlia lets me go from her embrace but her fingers stay firmly laced with mine as I pull my grandmama in tight for a long hug.

"I am sorry, I am so sweaty," I pant and she laughs.

"I am so proud of you. Your mom and dad must be screaming somewhere and bursting with pride. Oh, honey, you were amazing."

"Alexa, you need to go for your final check-in,"

Andy says with a smile, and I reluctantly untangle myself from hugs.

"How did I do, coach?" I ask with a wry smile and he offers me the biggest of compliments he has ever given me.

"You did the best in the world, Alexa."

∼

I get through the post-race procedures in an absolute daze and I am riding cloud nine. Without the officials, I am not sure I would even be in the right place. Andy is in his element. The sponsorships will come now. The deals. The prize money. The international paid-for meets. Olympics. Worlds. The doors just opened to a world-record-holding athlete.

I can't keep up with who is who so I don't bother to try. I just let each congratulation wash over me and I live in that moment. In that second.

If I hadn't... If I had been more alert... more observant of the world around me, I may have noticed the turn in the tides. The change of direction. But I was oblivious.

I emerge from the official area, showered, changed, and able to just about walk again, and make my way to the family enclosure. I have never been a winner in a race so big so as I feel the flash of cameras and the surge in attention from the media corner I bask in it, bathe in the attention as tomorrow my win would only be yesterday's news.

It is Andy who notices first. But not quick enough.

I hear the call of my name; the beckoning of a Sky reporter and I make my way over. Prepared to answer about my tactics, about how it felt to be a winner, who I wanted to thank, my inspiration. I don't process the question at first. But I feel the scramble of movement. Eyes on me. Shouts from the press

"Dahlia Dante..."

"How long..."

"Lovers?!"

"An Item..."

"Is it true that..."

"Are you gay? Is Dahlia Dante gay?"

I falter, my entire face changes. I stutter and I can't find my words. How do they know? What will Dahlia think? I didn't tell anyone. I spin on the ball of my foot and search for her. I spot her instantly with Mr. Suit, head down, cap in place, glasses on, being ushered out of the stands.

My grandmama is in shock, unsure what is going on around her as security piles in for Dahlia. I see them push by her and I feel angry, heat rises, who do they think they are?

I turn from the reporters and make my way to the enclosure.

"Grandmama! It's okay!" I call but she can't hear me. "Hey! Get out of my way!" I shout at some guy in a suit standing in my path trying to keep me from the pathway up.

"Sorry, ma'am. I can't let you through at this time for security reasons."

But my rational senses have gone and I start to push through.

"Yes, I know because that is Dahlia Dante up there with my Grandmama. Now. Let. Me. Through."

I push and push against him but he is an immovable object. Unwilling in any way to let me through as the commotion breaks out all around us. The reporters have seen Dahlia and they swarm over, the lights flash, the calls and shouts echo. My eyes dart between her and my Grandmama who is sitting back in her seat but she looks deathly pale.

I can't see Dahlia's face from the angle but the

stadium screen shows her in full view as she tries to escape, hiding herself the best she can but failing on all accounts.

A reporter pushes through the barricade and gets to her. His voice is loud and clear and it echoes in my brain.

"Dahlia! Are you in a lesbian relationship with newworld record holder Alexa Sharpe?!"

She pauses and the camera pans. It catches her mid-thought and I see it. A whirl of emotions. The possibilities that flash through her mind.

She could end this now; she could be true to herself and start the next chapter of her life free from lies and hiding who she is. I don't need to be locked away in her penthouse. We would have a chance. A real chance at a future together.

I reach for her with all of my being, mentally telling her it will be okay, that we can do this, she can do this. She has me. She leans into the microphone and I wait with bated breath.

"Oh honey," she says with a drawl, in a tone I barely recognize. "I don't date the wait staff."

17

Is it possible to feel the highest you have ever felt in your entire life whilst ultimately crushed from the inside out?

The moments immediately after Dahlia's one-line wonder are only a blur now. I think my mind blocked them out for my own mental health and sanity. I think I fell. Andy was there. Grandmama was brought to me and she gave me the most ferocious talking to I had ever had from her in my life.

"You are about to get on that podium and take your one and only gold medal. Don't let that circus take that away from you, Alexa. Promise me!"

I nodded and I tried. I tried to put the world out of my mind and enjoy that moment as it came.

As the British National Anthem chimed around the stadium, my head surpassed my heart in thought and I took my victory with pride and a Union Jack flag around my shoulders.

I let the tears stream down my cheeks as I dipped my head and felt the weight of gold medal. I had longed for this; I had spent my whole life working for this and yet it was tainted by her huge public betrayal.

The taste in my mouth was of bittersweet regret.

There was a celebration; I was there but also not there. I felt numb and could barely stop crying. Luckily most people just thought the gold medal had brought tears of joy and I let them think that. I sought out the news at every turn and watched the media circus unfold. I couldn't go home; the media were there. I was politely put on leave from my job, which I think would have been terminated immediately had I not just won the European Gold. They camped outside Grandmama's house for a few days but they got nothing, not even a twitch of a curtain.

I couldn't face what would need to happen next. I knew an ending with Dahlia was coming. I knew that the day we started, but the moment we had murmured the words *I love you*... I guess I had naively gained hope for a different ending for us. Then, even without the promise of a happily ever after I had, in turn, hoped for something better than this. A drifting apart, perhaps. Lives moving in different directions. Stolen moments as we both now traveled across the world. She for her movies and me for my races.

That was all gone now and I had never felt so stupid. Of course, I had only ever been the barmaid. The woman paid to help. Dahlia had never loved me; it was clear now. Lust, yes, she had been swept up in a wave of lust and passion but love? The real love that could change a person's path, alter the trajectory of their lives, overcome any barriers?

We had never had that.

Or if we had it, she burned it down with her southern sassy drawl that cut me to the bone.

Grandmama didn't ask any questions. She pieced together the series of events from the socialite news bulletins. I avoided them but it was impossible to miss. Dahlia's initial rejection of our encounter had stemmed the flow but failed to stop the bleed. The gossips didn't let go quite so easily, and before long, there were more and more snippets, quotes, photos.

Many of them were of me in the hotel, which was nothing new. I worked there. One of me in her car. One of us hugging when I won gold.

So, she made another statement. Yes, we knew each other. Yes, we were friends but nothing more. Acquaintances if anything, and she had taken an interest in my career, admired my talent on the track. She hadn't realized I was a lesbian. She hadn't realized that supporting me must have meant she must be in a mad lesbian affair with me...

My only comfort was that these were released as text statements. I didn't need to hear her say those words about me. I didn't need to hear her voice denying me over and over again. I only had to see them written on the screen. Repeated over and over again.

The only contact we had—if it could be called contact—was the delivery of my belongings to my grandmama's. Although I wouldn't say they were mine to begin with. Boxes of sports gear that I had worn once. Lingerie that had been purchased for long nights and lazy days. None of these things belonged to me, Alexa Sharpe. They all belonged to a woman who no longer existed... The version of Alexa who loved Dahlia Dante.

The other delivery was to my bank account. A large six-figure sum. It came with a note, that even though the terms of our agreement were not fully adhered to Ms. Dante insisted on the payment. I didn't touch the money, though. The very thought of it disgusted me.

I had signed a contract. It was full of rules and conditions and scenarios. It didn't tell me what to do when I fell in love with her. It wasn't a contract for love.

The only thing that I had left, the only thing that I could cling to, was my sport, my running. So, I dove in once more. Andy floated the idea that I should look for a new coach, that he wasn't good enough to train me through the next stages of my career.

My life was changing. From the extra publicity with the Dahlia thing, combined with my gold medal and new world record time, I was suddenly a big deal. I had signed a huge sponsorship program with a brand I couldn't afford a few weeks ago. They had given me a PA to organize my meets, my calendar was now full of training, meetings, travel, endorsements, photoshoots, appearances.

The hotel didn't need to wait until the storm passed to fire me. I quit before they had the chance. I wrote an email to Milly telling her I wouldn't be back to the house so she could take whatever she wanted and sell the rest. She didn't reply and I wasn't that surprised.

Grandmama had constant worry etched into her kind features. I hated myself for aging her, for making her feel all this stress. It was the last thing I wanted, but the sadness, the intense feeling of loss... I just couldn't shake it. I carried it around with me in everything I did. I felt like it would slow me down, that I must be running slower, that I had lost everything.

But the opposite was true. The slower I felt inside, the faster I ran. I was running the best I ever had in my life. No one could catch me, no one could even come close and I clung to that; it was the only anchor I had left.

Of course, I rang Dahlia. Or at least I tried. In the middle of the night when I could feel her skin on me, taste her on my tongue, feel the tangle of her limbs with mine... My heart denied me the sanity of clear thought and argued with me that what happened wasn't true.

I felt again like our love was real as the

moments of infinite tenderness we had shared were vivid in my mind. That Dahlia Dante had said she loved me too and meant it.

So, I called her. I text her. Again and again and again. But she never answered. And then, a few weeks later the phone never even rang. The texts didn't deliver. The line just cut to disconnected and that is when I knew for sure.

It was over. Dahlia Dante had moved on, so I had to find a way to, too.

18

I felt like a reluctant participant in my own story, living in the grey and watching from the sidelines. I was numb to it all—no highs, no lows, just existing. I think I could have continued like that forever, but I was not alone.

My grandmama gave me a month. A month of mourning and she told me that was more than fair.

"Look, Alexa, you have had your heart broken. You fell in love with a woman who just wasn't ready to love you. I feel for you, I have never felt that. I only know love ending because it was time to end and even then, it carried on in my heart. But she didn't choose that path. For you, I am angry but for her, I feel sad, she must be very lonely in her life. Far more alone than you can ever be because you have people who love you... for you. But more importantly than that, you love yourself and you have stayed true to yourself. That is not the easy path, but the one you chose and I admire you for that."

I feel the tears in my eyes rise and the sniffles begin. I'm not much of a crier. Mainly because I look awful when I cry, and whilst my life isn't usually all sunshine and rainbows, I also don't have a lot to cry about. I'm generally a happy person.

But I am heartbroken, I am hurt and upset, and sometimes I think we are told by society that it's wrong to feel those things. That bitterness and anger and sadness should be hidden and we should not indulge our pain.

But pain doesn't work like that, not for me anyway. I can't just push it to the side and forget about it, but I can face it and confront it and try to move forwards.

"I didn't know it could feel like what we had together. And now she is gone... it's like a limb is missing from me. There is a constant ache. I ache for her. All the time."

I feel the frail arms of an old woman wrap

around me and a tightness to her hug that shows just how much strength she still has in her. "I think it will ache for a long time, Alexa. I really do, but you have to try and look forwards now. You have so much happening around you. All you ever dreamed of is yours to have and you are missing it. And I don't think you want that for yourself. I know I most certainly don't want it for you. And neither would your mom and dad."

I nod. I know she is right, and the moment she mentions their names I feel a longing for them. I wish they were here. I need a hug from my dad, I need my mom to tell me everything will be okay.

"I am sorry, Grandmama, I need to get out. I'm going to go for a run. I just need to feel them close to me."

She pulls away and gives me a final last squeeze and a warm nod. I pull on my shoes and am out the door in a matter of seconds. I hear her mutter that they are always here for me to feel, but I need to go to our place. I need to be where I felt them the most.

∼

I take the bus out of the suburbs and further into the countryside. I could have run. It's about 22k round trip, which sounds a lot but it is doable for me. I just didn't want to run this time.

Oh honey, I don't date the wait staff.

I hear it over and over in my head. How could she say that about me?

Her voice is in my head over and over and over. Her words cut me to the bone each and every time.

Like the song you hate the most constantly on repeat on the radio. And the more you hear it, the less it makes sense. It loses its quality; the words lose their meaning, and yet you can't stop listening over and over until you drive yourself insane.

She doesn't date the wait staff, sure.

But she fucked me with a raw and open passion. We loved with an overwhelming completeness that I have never felt in my life.

When she knelt for me, I felt complete, when she kissed me, I was whole.

And now... now I am just the wait staff.

The bus stops about a mile away from the lake edge and I get off in a daze. Luckily, the weather is kind. A warm evening makes way for the setting sun and rising moon. I have an hour until the bus returns. Or two if I take too long, but there wouldn't be another after that.

I saunter along the road. Not a pace I'm accustomed to but all I had the energy for. Not physically but mentally.

I wonder if it's been a mistake coming here the moment the water comes into view. Because for the first time in my life, it isn't my parents that I feel here, it is Dahlia. Beautiful Dahlia. My Dahlia. Seeing her face again, the moment she first saw the sparkles ripple along the surface of the water. Her smile lit up the morning as she turned to me...

Yes, she had taken this place and made it hers too. Well, it seems that way now, although at that moment it felt as though I had given it to her. I would have given her anything. I look across the lake and I see our place. Our spot. My butterfly moment.

I move like a magnet, there is no way I could go anywhere else. Taking the path for what would be the last time. I wouldn't come back here now; it was time to lay memories to rest. But I needed my last goodbye.

As my feet find familiar meadow grass, I sink like a stone in the sea. My fingers run through the soft green shoots and claw at them. Desperate for a handful of something. I need to just feel something...

"Alexa."

Her voice comes to me like the sweetest taste of sugar in dark bitter tea. It cuts through the wind and I feel it on my skin.

I turn my head.

She isn't a figment of my imagination. She is real. She is here.

I can't look at her. I sob. I sob so loudly I'm sure the birds pity me. Tormented by my own memories and the voices in my head.

"Oh, Alexa," she says louder, with more need and passion and I can't take it. I want to scream.

And then I feel her. The softest touch of her fingertips at my shoulder. She's hesitant. Afraid. But she still sinks down beside me in the grass. I can't look at her, only at her knees, and watch as her graceful fingers reach for mine. She takes them in her palms holding them with a gentle caress. Waiting with all the time in the world for my breathing to slow and my body to turn to her.

"Don't. Don't, Dahlia. Don't come here because you pity me. I can't take it. I will be okay. I will get better. But you should go."

I don't know why I push her away, rejecting her

attention and affection when it is all I crave and want. Self-preservation perhaps. I move away from her, still avoiding looking into her eyes, not wanting to see that pity.

But she doesn't let go. She only holds on tighter.

"I'm not here for pity, Alexa. You can tell me to go. You have every right to hate me for what I have done to us, to you. But I am not here because I feel sorry for you. I am here because I love you and I can't live without you."

It takes a moment for my mind to process the words. And even when I do, I am not sure I believe them.

"Look at me," she begs, and I comply this time, turning towards her and casting my gaze over those pools of brilliant green. "I panicked. I was afraid and I did what I knew how to do. Deny. Move on. Forget. Except I can't forget you. I have been coming here every day for weeks hoping you would come. I didn't want to go to your grandmother's house. I thought she might kill me anyway and I would deserve no less. But I thought if you came here, then maybe you still loved me, maybe you could forgive what I did at the track…"

"But af-after you said... You said all of those things..." She looked at me angrily.

"Of course, I didn't say those things! That was Mr. Suit who kept putting out denial statements against my will and took my phone away. I fired him after I made him send you your money. I would never say those things about you, Alexa. How could you think that?!"

I look at her with incredulity.

"Okay, so I understand why you might think I said them. I know what I said about you to the cameras and I will regret that moment and the pain that it caused you for the rest of eternity. But I didn't continue denying you. Us. I haven't been able to function without you. I haven't left our penthouse. I know the media says I went back to the US, but it isn't true. I have been there the whole time. I have stalked you. I have you on google alerts, I tracked your air pods. I am crazy, I know. I am a crazy woman. You can end this if you want. I won't blame you at all. But I have to tell you. I have to tell you that I have never felt this way for anyone. I don't want to spend another day without you. Not another moment. I love you, Alexa Sharpe. And, I'm ready to come out to the world. I am so sorry for what I said and did to us.

I'm so sorry for what I did to you. If you give us another chance, this time it is real and forever. I promise you that. No hiding. No secrets. No contracts."

"No contract for love?"

She shakes her head and her eyes are full of hope.

I'm so angry with her and I can't believe she let me feel this way for weeks. Why she didn't she come to me sooner? There is so much we need to talk about. So much we need to work through. So much that needs to change.

But it also doesn't matter. Not really. I know we will find a way.

"I love you, Dahlia, my butterfly."

And as I feel her lips against mine, my heart and head are finally on the same page once more.

I had spent so long hoping for a happy ending. But little did I know that when it came, it would be just the beginning.

The End

EPILOGUE
5 YEARS LATER

Life has a funny way of working out. From the moment Dahlia kissed me at the lake, my life took on another change. Well, it was already changing thanks to my newly acquired gold medal and world record, but now it was a step into the spotlight.

I forgave Dahlia for her words that broke me. We all fuck up sometimes and she has spent her whole life denying her sexuality and hiding huge parts of herself. She reacted to the press questions like a hunted animal. She used her acting skills to say what she had been trained forever to say. Denial.

She doesn't deny any more. She embraces our love in every way and we are very open about it.

Luckily, I am boring and Dahlia's new manager, Giselle, who I instantly adored, wasted no time in telling our story to the world. The real story.

She wiped away all the bad practices of Mr. Suit and before you knew it, the public was eating out of Dahlia's palm again, only this time it was real and I think that made it better for everyone. Being a lesbian actress was not such a terrible thing anymore as it was all those years ago for Dahlia in the movie industry. Okay, a Christian Southern gay woman... a little more PR needed, but I was *wholesome* as Giselle liked to put it. My life was something people warmed to, they saw me and Grandmama, how hard I had worked in my career, and how I had now made this beautiful woman happy and they came round to the idea.

They just didn't know the things we got up to in the bedroom. Then again, they would probably like that, too.

As for me, I got my big chance and went to the Olympics to represent Great Britain the following year. I was on the form of my life and I was never in doubt that I would win there. I went into the final as the favorite. I ran my own race and I won the Olympic gold medal, almost easily, and felt overwhelmed and at peace all at the same time.

For so many years, I had thought I would never quite be good enough. I had always been the one who finished 8th, 5th, sometimes even squeezed a bronze medal. I had almost accepted that, that I was the 'nearly' runner. The one that was close, but never quite close enough.

I'll never know exactly what made the difference to my times. I actually think it was Dahlia. In loving Dahlia, I had found a fierce passion inside of me that translated to my racing. I suddenly had a harder edge to me that came with the fullness with which I was experiencing the rest of my life.

Even in the time I lost Dahlia, I was feeling extremes of emotions I never thought possible and I poured all that feeling into racing.

Grandmama is still alive and mostly doing well. We spend a lot of time together when I am in London.

Dahlia and I have both traveled a lot, but it is becoming less and less for both of us. I am getting too old to race, so I have chosen to retire as a champion. I currently hold the Olympic, World and European Golds, but I won't be defending them.

Andy and I have been working hard on a training academy and developing a youth program to support the next generation of young girls- track athletes, just like me who have talent, but no funding to take their athletic career to the next level.

I feel excited about it, and it keeps me grounded. It is easy to forget where I came from sometimes when I am around Dahlia's lifestyle for too long. And if she has too much time in England, she gets the *rain blues* as she calls them and will jet off to Texas for a taste of the sun.

All in all, we are not perfect.

But we are honest, happy, open and in love.

We speak often about the future, about settling down properly in a forever home that will likely be somewhere in the US.

For now and for the rest of Grandmama's life, our home is in London. We have a beautiful town house in Kensington with an incredible roof terrace. I like to run in Hyde Park every morning.

We are getting a dog now I'm not travelling any more. I have always loved dogs, but just wanted to be able to give a dog a lovely home and I know I can do that now.

Dahlia wondered if we might get a perfectly

coiffed pedigree dog, but that isn't what I want and she is happy to indulge me. I am scouring dog rescue places for a big cuddly bear of a dog that needs a loving home. I will take our dog everywhere with me and I can't wait.

We both have our passions in life that we still follow, although Dahlia is much more choosy about projects that she will take on, now. She will only act in something if she really believes in it and in the director. It has given her much more interesting roles and I love watching what it has brought out in her on the screen.

She obviously still has her Dahlia Dante magic. Her star quality is shining brighter than it ever has and the roles she is offered are bigger than ever.

Whether it is through love or through having Giselle as her agent instead of Mr Suit, who knows?

When we are alone together, we still have that magic. We still fit together effortlessly and comfortably in a way I have never felt with anyone and I know unequivocally that she is mine. I mean 'mine' in a possessive sense, but I will never try to cage her free spirit.

When I look at her sleeping form in crisp

white sheets as the morning light creeps through our big bay windows, I feel infinite tenderness for her.

This is what our love looks like and I can't imagine anything better.

THANK YOU FOR READING

Thank you so much for reading this story. I really hope you loved Alexa and Dahlia as much as I loved writing them.

I am a huge movie lover and the chance to write about a famous actress was a big lure for me. I always wonder about the women we see on the big screen. We fall for their public persona and their star quality, but what are they really like? What is it really like to be one of the most famous and recognisable women in the world?

And what is it like to be one of those women and to have secrets and made sacrifices throughout their career?

Thank you for reading

If you liked this book, please do check out the next book in the Infinite Tenderness series for more! mybook.to/IT2

FREE BOOK

Pick up my book, Summer Love for FREE when you sign up to my mailing list.

On a beach in France, Summer crashes into Max's life and changes everything. This is a hot and heady summer romance. https://BookHip.com/MFPGZAX

My mailing list is the best place to be the first to find out about new releases, Free books, special offers and price drops. You'll also find out a bit about my life and the inspiration behind the stories and the characters. Oh, and you'll love Summer Love. :)

ALSO BY MARGAUX FOX

Her Royal Bodyguard Series

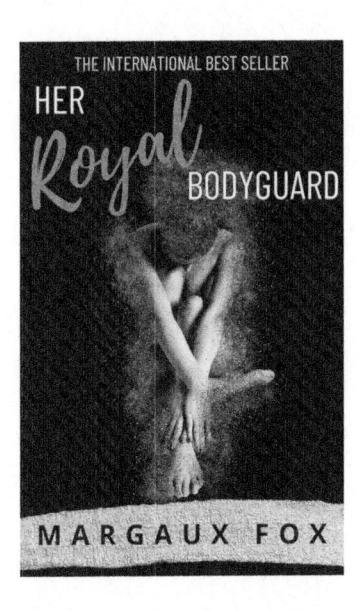

Erin is the Princess's Bodyguard. The last thing that is supposed to happen is that she falls in love with her.
getbook.at/HRB

Printed in Great Britain
by Amazon